THE COYOTE

THE COYOTE

Robert J. Horton

CHIVERS

British Library Cataloguing in Publication Data available

This Large Print edition published by BBC Audiobooks Ltd, Bath, 2010.
Published by arrangement with Golden West Literary Agency.

U.K. Hardcover ISBN 978 1 408 47752 6
U.K. Softcover ISBN 978 1 408 47753 3

Printed and bound in Great Britain by
CPI Antony Rowe, Chippenham and Eastbourne

CONTENTS

CHAPTER ONE

REWARDS OFFERED

The sign on the tree attracted the man's attention while he was still far down the slope. He could see the tall pine on the crest of the ridge above a veritable landmark in that country of stunted timber, and the square of paper, tacked to its trunk under the lowest branches, gleamed white against the background of vivid green.

The air was clear, and every detail of the landscape—the red rocks, the saffron-colored slopes, the green pines and firs and buck brush, the white cliffs—everything within sight for miles stood out, clean-cut in the brilliant sunshine which flooded the empty land under a cloudless sky.

When the man, mounted on a lean, dun-colored horse, first looked up at a turn of the narrow trail and saw the sign, he grunted. Then he frowned and looked back along the way he had come with a glowing light of reflection in his gray eyes. He was a tall man, slim and muscular, clean-shaven, his face and hands bronzed by sun and wind, and his face open and good-natured. A shock of blond hair showed where his gray, wide-brimmed, high-crowned hat was pushed back from his high

1

forehead.

His dress, though typical of the country which he traversed, was distinctive, or it might have been a certain natural grace that made it seem so. He wore a light-gray, soft shirt made of French flannel, a dark-blue silk scarf, leather chaps over olive-drab khaki trousers, black, hand-sewed riding boots which displayed their polish despite a coating of fine dust, silver spurs, and, strapped to his right thigh, was a worn leather holster, natural color, from which protruded the black butt of a six-gun.

On the back of his saddle was tied a black slicker, the raincoat of the open country, which bulged with a medium-sized pack done up within it.

One would have taken him to be thirty, perhaps a year or two more when his face was serious; but when he smiled, that is, when he smiled naturally, he looked little more in years than a youth who has just attained his majority.

When he smiled the other smile—the smile he now expressed as he looked up the slope toward the tall pine with the white square of paper on its trunk—one would have forgotten the smile because of the sinister, steel-blue look in his eyes, and the direct, piercing quality of his gaze.

He walked his horse up the winding trail. His right foot was clear of the stirrup, and he swung it idly. His left hand, in which he held the reins, rested lightly on the horn of his saddle, and his right gripped the cantle at his back. He hummed a ditty of the desert, but his gaze, keen and alert, continually sought the open stretches of trail above him, and at regular intervals flashed back along the way he had come.

In time he reached the top of the ridge and pulled up his horse near the tree bearing the poster. He dismounted and walked slowly up a little grade to where he could the better read the legend on the paper.

It was printed in large letters, but recent rain had somewhat faded it.

FIVE HUNDRED DOLLARS REWARD
This will be paid for
THE COYOTE
dead or alive, by San Jacinto County.
JUDSON BROWN, J. P.,
Dry Lake.

This man is tall and light in complexion, gray or blue eyes, good teeth, his horse said branded CC2, keeps himself neat, dangerous with gun, squints when mad. Bring him in and get the money.

The man swore softly as he read the last sentence. 'Bring him in an' get the money,' he

3

said snortingly. 'You'd think they was talkin' about a locoed steer that just had to be roped an' drug, or shot an' hauled. Bring him in an' get the money!'

There was genuine indignation in his tone as he repeated the offensive sentence.

'Well, it can't be me,' he said facetiously, aloud. 'My name's Rathburn—a right good name.' His eyes clouded. 'A right good name till they began to tamper with it,' he muttered with a frown as he lit a cigarette he had built while perusing the placard.

He took the stub of a lead pencil from the pocket of his shirt. For some moments he reflected, staring at the sign on the tree trunk. Then he laboriously printed on its lower edge:

Five thousand dollars more from the State of Arizona if you can get it.

Rathburn surveyed his work with a grin, replacing the pencil in his shirt pocket. Then he stepped back and drew his gun. He seemed on the point of sending a half dozen bullets through the paper when he suddenly shook his head, glanced hurriedly about him, and shoved the weapon back into its sheath.

He walked quickly to his horse, swung into the saddle, and started down the trail on the western side of the ridge.

Below him he saw a far-flung vista of rounded, yellow hills, spotted with the green of small pines and firs. The ground was hard, dry, and gravelly. There were boulders a-plenty, and long, sharp-edged outcroppings of hard rock of a reddish hue. There was no sign of habitation to be glimpsed from the trail leading down from the high ridge which he had crossed. He continually looked about him with the interested air of a man who is venturing into a new locality with which he is not familiar.

'Dry lake!' he exclaimed, while his horse pricked up its ears at the familiar voice. 'Good name for it, if it's anywhere in *this* country. Hoss, I don't know when we're gain' to drink again. I didn't figure on hittin' a desert up here.'

He rode on at a brisk jog, down and down the winding trail. Then it led across a number of the round, low hills, ever westward.

As the afternoon wore on, more green brightened the landscape and patches of grass appeared. Then they came upon a small stream trickling down from the higher slopes to northward where horse and rider drank their fill and rested in a quiet, secluded meadow off the trail.

The man's face was a study as he lay back upon the grass in the cool shade of a clump of pines. Whimsical and wistful, it was occasionally lit by a peculiar smile which carried a hint of sadness. His eyes half closed, dreamily. The smoke from his cigarette curled

5

upward in a thin spiral in the still air of the altitudes. His horse, with reins dangling and saddle cinch loosened, cropped the grass which carpeted the meadow.

Finally the man arose, tightened the cinch in an absent manner, mounted, and rode back to the trail to continue on his way. At the top of the next ridge he halted, looking at a little ranch which lay in a wide valley a mile or two north of the thread of trail which he could see winding westward. The place looked poor, poverty-stricken, despite the small field of living green south of the house and the few head of cattle grazing along the banks of a little stream which wound through the valley.

For some time the rider sat his horse motionless, frowning in indecision. Then he touched the dun lightly with his spurs, left the trail, and struck off to the north, following the ridge. He kept his gaze focused on the little ranch. The only sign of life which he saw was a heavily-burdened clothesline flapping in the idle breeze which at this point was wafted down from the mountains.

When he was almost directly above the small house he turned his mount down the slope and gaining the floor of the valley, rode at a gallop for the house. His right hand now rested on his thigh near the holstered gun.

As he brought his horse to a stop near the front of the house a girl appeared in the doorway. He looked at her in pleased surprise.

Then his hat swept low in a gesture of courtesy.

'Ma'am, I've found this to be a country of scattered habitations,' he said in a musical bass. 'So when I glimpsed your abode from yonder hills I said to myself, "Rathburn, you're most powerful hungry; maybe you better pay a call."'

His eyes were glowing with an amused light, and a pleasant smile played upon his lips.

The girl, who had listened curiously, now laughed in welcome. 'There aren't many places between here and Dry Lake,' she said; 'and I guess it would be a pretty hot ride today. You can water your horse—and feed him at the barn, if you wish—and I'll get you something to eat, if you're not particular.' Her eyes danced merrily.

'Ma'am!' he exclaimed, with mock severity, 'I quit bein' particular when I was—when I was as young as that youngster.'

A boy of ten or twelve had appeared beside the girl.

'Young man, what're those dirt-looking spots on your face?' asked the stranger, frowning with his eyes but smiling with his lips.

'They *ain't* dirt spots!' returned the boy with spirit, advancing a step.

'No?' said the man, feigning intense astonishment. 'What *are* they?'

'They're freckles,' answered the boy stoutly.

'Oh—oh, *that's* what they are,' said the

7

stranger with a delighted laugh. 'Won't they wash off?'

'Naw. You can't fool me. You knew what they were!'

'Well, now, maybe so,' observed the man as the girl laughingly turned inside.

'Grub'll be ready by time you are,' she called back to him.

'I'll show you where to put your horse,' said the boy as the man looked searchingly up and down the valley.

CHAPTER TWO

A BOY AND A GIRL

When Rathburn had put up his horse, after giving him a light feed of grain in the barn, he followed the boy to the rear of the house where he found water, soap, and a towel on a bench, above which hung a small mirror.

The boy left him there, and he soon washed and combed his hair. The girl opened the rear door for him and he walked through the little kitchen into a small front room where a table was set for him.

'Sure, ma'am, I didn't figure on causing you so much trouble,' he said with a smile. 'I didn't expect anything but a snack, an' here you've gone an' fixed a regular dinner—this time of

8

day, too.'

'My experience with men in this country has taught me that when they're hungry, they're hungry,' replied the girl. 'And it wasn't much trouble. Those beans were in the oven and already warm. I just had to make the coffee. I was expecting my brother.'

'I didn't see any men around the place,' he said, beginning to eat. 'If I had I'd have made myself known to them before coming to the house. Where is he—out with the cattle?'

He saw her gaze was troubled. 'I don't know just where he is—today,' she confessed. 'He goes away and sometimes doesn't come back for a day or two.' She stood in the doorway.

Rathburn noted her trim, slim figure and her wealth of chestnut hair. She was pretty and capable. He surmised that her parents were dead, although he could not ascribe the reason for this deduction. Evidently the boy was a younger brother. He wondered if the older brother would return before he finished eating.

'How far is it to Dry Lake?' he asked casually.

'Oh—why didn't you come from there?' She seemed surprised.

'No. I came from over to eastward.'

'But it's miles and miles to any place east of here, isn't it?' she asked, puzzled. 'You must have had a long ride.'

A ghost of a frown played on his brows.

Then he laughed. 'Yes, miss, I've been ridin' some,' he confessed. 'I didn't know how far it was to anywhere or I mightn't have come in this direction.'

She looked at him wonderingly, and again he thought he saw a troubled look in her eyes.

'You're going to Dry Lake?' she asked.

'Yes,' he said shortly, and a grim note crept into his voice. 'It's west of here, ain't it?'

'About fifteen or eighteen miles,' she answered. 'The trail leads there from the lower end of this valley—the same trail you came on, I guess. Are you a cow-puncher?'

'Don't I look like one, miss?'

'Yes, you do and—you don't.' She was confused by the quality of his smile. But his eyes seemed to glow at her kindly, with a cheerful, amused light—altogether honest and friendly. She lowered her gaze and flushed despite herself.

'My vocation, miss—you're too young an' pretty to be called ma'am, if you'll excuse me for saying so—is a peculiar one. I've punched cows, yes; I've prospected an' worked a bit in the mines. I've scared the wolf from the "Welcome" mat by standing off the boys at green-topped tables, an' once I—I—worked on a sort of farm.' He appeared apologetic as he confessed this last. 'I guess I wasn't cut out for a farm hand, miss.'

She laughed at this. 'Are you going to work in Dry Lake?' she asked, sobering.

'Well, now, that is a question,' he returned, draining his cup of the last of the coffee.

'I'll get you some more,' she said quickly, taking his cup. 'Dry Lake isn't a very big place, you know.'

'Just how big is Dry Lake?' he asked when she returned from the kitchen with more coffee for him.

'Only a hundred or two. But the men from miles and miles go there because—because there are places there where they can stand the wolf off at the green-topped tables and— drink.' The troubled look was in her eyes again. 'Sometimes the wolf catches up with them before they get home,' she added, smiling faintly.

'It's not a safe system,' he said thoughtfully.

'But you might get work in Dry Lake,' she said hopefully. 'You—you look capable. The cattlemen from back in the hills go there and they're nearly always looking for men, I've heard. You might meet some of them and get a job.'

He beamed upon her. 'I've always heard that a woman gave a man encouragement an' ambition, if she was a good one,' he mused. 'You've almost got me thinking I'd better go straight to work.'

'Why—didn't—wasn't that your intention?' she asked wonderingly.

His face clouded. 'It ain't always so easy for me to do what I want to do, miss,' he said. 'I—

11

you see—' He broke off his speech with a frown. 'This is a queer country, miss,' he said earnestly.

'Oh, I know,' she said eagerly. 'I'll bet you're an—an officer!'

Then he laughed. It was the spontaneous laugh of youth, vibrant, compelling, mirth-inspiring.

'Say, miss, if there's one thing I ain't tackled yet, it's being an officer,' he chuckled as he finished his repast.

She smiled vaguely, studying him under her long, dark lashes. The boy came into the room, holding his hands behind him, and stood with his sturdy legs braced apart, staring at Rathburn.

'There he is now!' Rathburn exclaimed. 'Did you try to wash the freckles off?' he queried with a wink.

'I know who *you* are!' said the boy. There was admiration and awe in his wide eyes.

Rathburn looked at him closely, his brows wrinkling.

'Yes, I do,' said the boy, nodding. 'Did he tell you who he is, sis?' he asked, looking at the girl.

'Now, Frankie, we don't care who the man is,' she reproved. 'He was hungry and he's welcome. What's the matter with you?'

'I guess you'd be surprised if you knew as much as I do,' the boy boasted. 'I guess you'd be surprised all right. I do.'

'I've been surprised more than once at things you knew,' the girl said with a laugh.

'Yes, but I guess you'd be surprised all right if you knew who *he* is,' cried the boy, pointing at Rathburn.

'Come, now, young fellow, don't be getting all het up here,' said Rathburn slowly, drawing tobacco and papers from his shirt pocket. 'What do you find to do with yourself around here?'

But the youngster was not to be diverted from his topic. 'I was lookin' at your horse,' he said, his eyes shining. 'That's how I know for sure an' certain who you are.'

Rathburn gazed at the boy sternly as he touched a match to his brown-paper cigarette. 'My horse is all right, ain't he?'

'Sure he is,' said the boy eagerly. 'I bet he can go some, too. He'd have to go for you to have him, wouldn't he? You're The Coyote!'

Rathburn continued to smile with an amused tolerance. But the girl gave a start; her hands flew to her breast, and she stared at the man with wide-open eyes.

'Frankie! What are you saying?' she exclaimed. The boy triumphantly brought his hands from behind his back. He held out a poster.

'His horse has got CC2 for a brand, just like it says in this bill Ed brought from town!' he cried. 'He's The Coyote, all right. But I won't tell,' he added quickly, looking at Rathburn.

13

The man avoided the girl's eyes. The boy laid the poster on the table where she could read it again, word for word.

'Tall—light in complexion—gray or blue eyes—good teeth—horse branded CC2—dangerous—'

And this man was tall and blond, with gray eyes. Five hundred dollars reward!

'I won't tell anybody you've been here,' the boy continued. 'We won't tell, will we, sis?' He looked at the girl imploringly.

'My brother Ed says what you want you take,' said the boy, gazing at the man in admiration. 'An' he says you don't rob anybody that can't afford it! He says the banks are insured an' you've been a friend to more'n one that's just gettin' a start in the cattle. I won't tell anybody you've been here, an' I won't let sis tell anybody, either!'

Rathburn was smiling wistfully. 'Always tell the truth, sonny,' he said in a low voice. 'Don't forget that. I wouldn't want you to lie for me. Any man that would want you to lie for him wouldn't be a man a-tall, son. See?'

'But old Brown, the judge, or the sheriff might come along an' want to know if you'd been here!' said the boy in breathless excitement.

'Then tell 'em the truth,' said Rathburn smilingly. 'Tell 'em a man with a horse branded CC2 was here an' kidded you about your freckles, had something to eat, an' rode away. Don't lie, sonny, no matter what happens.'

The girl took a step toward the table. 'You—*are*—The Coyote?' she asked in a whisper.

'My name is Rathburn, miss,' he replied cheerfully. 'In some ways I'm a lot like the man described in that reward notice. An' I'm riding a dun-colored horse branded CC2. I don't like that monicker, Coyote, or I might 'fess up to it.'

'Then—if you're him—you're an outlaw!' she stammered.

Rathburn's dreamy look shifted to the boy who was staring at him.

'You'll grow up to be quite a man, son,' he said in a fatherly tone. 'Those freckles mean a tough skin. A weak sort of skin tans quick an' the toughest just sunburns. You're halfway between. That's all right for freckles; but it don't go in life. It's best to be on one side or the other, an' the right side's the best for most folks.'

He rose and went for his hat. Then he extracted a roll of bills from a hip pocket and laid a five-dollar note on the table.

'That meal was worth it,' he said to the girl with a smile.

She shook her head. 'I—I couldn't take it,' she said.

'That's clean money, miss. I earned it circumventin' three of the most ornery card

15

sharps in Arizona.'

She continued to shake her head. 'You do not understand,' she murmured. 'It—it wouldn't make any difference. We couldn't take money from a stranger who came to us—hungry. It wouldn't make any difference who you were.'

'Aw, we need it, sis!' blurted out the boy. 'The Coyote's all right. He wouldn't lie to us.'

Rathburn laughed and, stepping to the boy, ran his fingers in his hair. 'I guess I've made a friend,' he said in a wistful voice. Then he picked up the bill on the table and stuffed it into the boy's pocket. His eyes encountered the poster again and they clouded. He turned away from it.

'Miss, you'll let me thank you—sure.'

She nodded, retreating a few paces.

'Then I'll be going,' he said, stepping to the door.

'To—to Dry Lake?' she found the voice to ask.

'Yes. To Dry Lake.'

He left the house and in a few minutes reappeared from the direction of the barn, riding his dun-colored horse. He did not stop, but galloped down the valley, waving a hand in farewell which the boy answered.

The day was nearly spent. The sun was low in the west, sliding down like a ball of gold toward the rim of the blue mountains. A stiff breeze had sprung up, driving the heat before it. At the lower end of the valley Rathburn found the trail he had left when he detoured to the ranch. He turned westward upon it, put spurs to his horse, and sped toward town.

It was just as well that the girl could not see the look which came to his face as he rode into the sunset.

CHAPTER THREE

THE LAW

Night had descended when Rathburn came in sight of the little town on the edge of the foothills. He rode slowly toward it, staring moodily at the flickering lights between interlaced branches which waved and weaved in the wind blowing down from the mountains. In all the distance he had traveled from the lonely ranch where he had met the girl and the boy he had encountered no one. He surmised that the trail to the desert hills to eastward was not a popular one.

As he neared the town he saw that it consisted of one main street with buildings clustered about it, and numerous shacks scattered in the lee of the hills. There were trees close to the eastern end of the street which he was approaching, and when he reached these trees he dismounted, led his horse into the shadows, and tied it.

He walked down the main street, which was illuminated only by the stars and the yellow gleams of light from windows on either side.

There were several resorts, and one in particular seemed the most popular. Rathburn glanced in through the door of this place as he passed and saw that it consisted of a bar and numerous tables, where games were in progress. He did not stop but continued on his way.

Few people were on the street; none of them took any especial notice of him. Several doors below the largest resort which he had so casually investigated, he came to a small, one-story, white-painted building, which, save for the door and window in its front, looked like a huge box. Across the glass in the door was lettered in gold:

JUDSON BROWN
Justice of the Peace
Notary Public

A dim light shone within, and, peering through the window, Rathburn saw that this light came from a lamp in a second room behind the little front office.

He looked up and down the street and saw but two pedestrians, both walking up the other side of the thoroughfare with their back to him. He tried the door stealthily, found it unlocked, and stepped quickly inside. Three strides took him to the door of the inside room.

A man looked up from a small table where he was engaged in writing. He was a stout man, large of countenance, with small black eyes under bushy brows which were black, although his hair was gray. He scowled heavily at the intruder who failed to remove his hat, and who stood, with feet well apart, in the doorway, a whimsical smile playing on his lips.

In a sweeping glance Rathburn saw that the room contained a bed, wardrobe closet, several chairs, and other articles of furniture and decoration of a bedroom and living room. His eyes flashed back to the burly man sitting at the table, pen poised, coolly surveying him with a frown.

'Your name Jud Brown?' he asked, stepping inside the room and to the side of the door toward the table where he could not be seen from the street.

'I'm *Judge* Brown,' replied the large man testily. 'You should have knocked before you came in, but now you're here, state your business as quickly as possible.'

'That's a businesslike tone that I admire to hear, Brown,' drawled Rathburn. 'You'll excuse my not callin' you judge. I'm afraid when you find out who I am you'd think I was kiddin' you!'

He smiled amiably while the justice glared

19

angrily.

'You're drunk!' flared Brown. 'The best thing you can do is get out of here—quick.'

Rathburn looked pained. 'First you ask me to state my business an' now you tell me to get out,' he complained. 'You might as well know that I never touch likker,' he added convincingly.

Brown was studying him intently with a puzzled look on his face. 'Well,' he said finally, with a show of irritation, 'what do you want?'

'I want you to tell me the why an' the wherefores of this document,' said Rathburn sternly as he drew a folded piece of paper from a pocket and spread it out on the table before the astonished gaze of the justice.

'That's one of a number I saw tacked on trees on the east trail out of here,' continued Rathburn, frowning. 'What's it all about, Brown?'

The pen in the hand of the justice suddenly began to waver as the hand trembled. Then Brown dropped it, squared away his chair, and looked grimly at his nocturnal visitor. For some moments his gaze was concentrated on Rathburn's face. Then he slowly read the poster offering a reward of five hundred dollars for The Coyote. He wet his lips with his tongue.

'So I was right!' he exclaimed. 'You *were* headed in this direction. I'm assuming that you're The Coyote!'

'And you're assuming what's the bare, untarnished truth,' said Rathburn. 'I'm The Coyote you've offered five hundred for, an' who'll bring another five hundred in several counties in Arizona, not to mention five thousand that the State of Arizona has tossed into the pot. I suppose I'm worth at least ten thousand as I stand here.'

'That would be cheap for a man of your reputation!' said the justice bravely. 'We don't want you across the line in California, Coyote. We won't put up with your depredations, and if you murder one of our citizens you'll hang!'

Rathburn's chilling laugh hung upon the justice's words. 'You're side-stepping the point,' he said suddenly in crisp tones that were like the crack of a whiplash. 'You're anticipating events, Jud. That's my complaint—that's my business here with you.' He brought his right palm down upon the table smartly.

'An' now that I'm here, Jud, you're sure goin' to listen!'

'Don't threaten me!' cried the justice. 'There are a hundred men within call and they'd make short work of you if they got their hands on you. Darn your ornery hide, I'm holding the winning cards in this game!' he concluded excitedly.

Rathburn was smiling at him; and it was not his natural smile. It gave the justice pause as he looked up into those narrowed gray eyes, shot with a steel-blue light. Rathburn's right hand and wrist moved with incredible swiftness, and Brown found himself staring into the black bore of a six-gun. Still he saw the eyes above the weapon. His face blanched.

'There are six winning cards in my right hand,' Rathburn said slowly. 'You can start shoutin' for those hundred men you mentioned just as soon as you want. Brown, it's you an' your kind that's made me desperate—dangerous, like you said in that printed notice. I won't fool with you or any other man on earth!'

'What—what did you come here for?' stammered the justice.

'To get away from—from back there in that cactus-bordered country of black, lava hills where I was born an' where I belong!' said Rathburn grimly, sliding into a chair on the opposite side of the table from Brown.

'Listen to me! I was driven out. I've ridden for a week with the idea of gettin' where I wasn't known an' where I could maybe get a fresh start, and here I find a reward notice staring me in the face from the top of the first hill I cross after leaving Arizona. I've never been here before; I've done nothing to molest you or your town; but you sic the pack on me first off an' hard-running, without any reason, except that you've *heard* things about me, I reckon.'

Brown nodded his head as Rathburn

22

finished. A measure of composure returned to him. His eyes gleamed with cunning as he remembered that his front door was unlocked and some one might by chance come in. But he again felt troubled as he conjectured what might happen in such event.

'You cannot blame me,' he said to Rathburn. 'You've robbed, and you're a killer—'

'That's what you *hear*?' thundered Rathburn. 'I admit several robberies—holdups of crooked, gambling joints like you've got in this town, an' petty-larceny bankers who robbed poor stockmen with sanction of the law. I've killed one man who had it coming to him. But I've shouldered the blame for every killing an' every robbery that's been staged in the desert country for the last three years. 'The Coyote did it,' is what they say, an' the crooks an' gunmen that turned the deal go free. I'm talking to you, Brown, as man to man—a thing I've never done with any mouthpiece of the law before. I'm trying to show you how you an' your kind can make a man an outlaw an' keep him one till somebody shoots him down. I'm sore, Brown, because I know that one of these days I'm going to get it myself!'

The justice saw that the man was in deadly earnest. He saw the hand resting on the table tighten its grip upon the gun.

'I didn't know all these things,' he said hastily. 'I had to judge by what I heard—and

23

read. Why didn't you make all this known to the Arizona authorities?'

Rathburn laughed harshly. 'Because I'd be framed clear across the board,' he said jeeringly. 'It's the law! It's as much of a crime to rob a thieving gambler or a snake of a whisky runner or peddler as it is to rob a home! I've had to rob to live! An' all the while there's been the makings of one of the hardest-lookin' bad men that this Southwest country ever saw in me. And, now that I think of it, why the devil I've held off I don't know!'

Brown was moved by the sincerity of the man. He saw in Rathburn's eyes that he was speaking the gospel truth. He saw something else in those eyes—the yearning of a homeless, friendless man, stamped with the stigma of outlawry, rebelling against the forces which were against him, relentlessly hunting him down.

'You say you came here to start over?' he asked curiously. 'How do I know you won't walk right out of this office and turn a trick right here in this very town?'

'You don't know it, that's the devil of it!' exclaimed Rathburn. 'An' there's no use in my telling you I won't, for you wouldn't take my word for it. You've got me pegged for a gun-fightin' bandit of first water an' clear crystal, an' I won't try to wise you up because it wouldn't do any good. Now that you know I'm in this country, you'll blame the first wrong thing that happens on to me. I've got no business here talking to you. I'm wasting my breath. You'll have to find out from somebody besides me that I was telling you the truth, an' I reckon that coincidence ain't in the pictures. Where's your handcuffs?'

The justice stared at him, startled.

'Where's your handcuffs?' insisted Rathburn angrily.

'In the drawer of my desk out in front,' replied Brown.

'Go an' get 'em an' bring 'em here,' Rathburn commanded. 'I'll keep my drop on you under cover.'

Brown rose and went to his desk in the front room while Rathburn watched him in the doorway with his gun held under his coat.

When the justice returned to the inside room Rathburn moved a chair close against one of the bedposts. He compelled Brown to sit in the chair, put his hands around between the supports in the back, and about the bedpost. He handcuffed him in that position.

Drawing a bandanna handkerchief from a pocket he swiftly gagged the justice. Then he rummaged about the room until he found a piece of rope tied about a pack in the bottom of the wardrobe. With this he secured Brown's ankles to the front legs of the chair.

'There!' he said, standing back to view his handiwork. 'You're pretty well trussed up. I ain't trusting you any more than you'd trust

25

me, an' I don't figure on you raising any hue an' cry before I can get along on my way.'

The eyes of the justice were rolling as he struggled in vain to speak.

'Never mind,' said Rathburn. 'I reckon I know what you want to say. Under the circumstances, the same being so much on my side, you'd say you believed me an' all that. But I took a chance in coming here to tell you what I did an' I never aim to take more'n one chance in a day. So long.'

CHAPTER FOUR

'I KNEW HE LIED!'

Rathburn extinguished the light in the lamp, walked swiftly to the front door, and outside. Closing the door softly he turned back up the street. He sauntered along slowly, debating his next move. Evidently the town was the last for many miles in the mountainous country east and north. Westward he would come upon many towns as the country became more and more densely populated toward the coast. Northwestward he would be able to keep within the arm of the mountains and still be in touch with civilization. But he would have to make some changes in his attire and fix that brand on his horse.

Instinctively his course brought him to the big resort he had noticed upon his arrival. The entrance doors had been closed against the chill of the night, but he could see the interior of the place through one of the windows despite the coating of dust upon the glass.

As he peered within he stiffened to alert attention and a light oath escaped him. Walking swiftly from a rear door was a tall man, the lower part of his face concealed by a black handkerchief. He held a gun in each hand and was covering the score or more patrons of the place who had risen from the tables, or stepped back from the bar, with their hands held high above their heads.

'Keep 'em there an' you'll be all right,' the masked man was saying in a loud voice which carried to Rathburn through cracks in the window glass. 'Line up down there, now—you hear me? Line up!'

The patrons lined up, keeping their faces toward the bandit.

'If anybody gets to acting uneasylike it'll be the signal for me to start shootin'—understand?' came the holdup's menacing voice as he moved around behind the bar.

'Open both cash drawers,' he ordered the servitor in the white apron. He covered the bartender with one gun while he kept the other pointed in the direction of the men standing in line.

Obeying instructions, the bartender took

27

the bills from the cash drawers and laid them before the bandit on the bar. He then made several piles of silver near the bills, walking to and from the drawers of the big cash register. Continuing to do as he was told, he stuffed the bank notes and silver into the masked man's pockets, one gun's muzzle against his breast, the other holding the men in line at bay.

Rathburn heard footsteps on the walk close to him. He whirled and saw two men about to enter the resort. 'I wouldn't go in there,' he said sharply in a low voice.

'Eh—what's that?'

The two men paused, looking at him questioningly.

'I wouldn't go in there,' Rathburn repeated. 'Come here an' take a look.'

One of the men stepped to his side and peered curiously through the window.

'Bill!' he whispered excitedly. 'Look here. It's a holdup!'

The other man looked over his shoulder. He swore softly.

'I'll bet it's The Coyote!' said the first man in an awed voice.

'Probably is,' said Rathburn sneeringly. 'They say he was heading this way.'

'Good place to stay out of—if it's *him*,' declared the second man.

Rathburn suddenly pulled back his left sleeve. 'See that?' he said, pointing to his left forearm.

The two men stared at the bared forearm in the yellow light which shone through the dust-stained window. They saw a scar about three inches below the elbow.

'Looks like a bullet made that,' one of the men observed.

'You're right,' said Rathburn, letting down his shirt sleeve. 'A bullet from The Coyote's gun left that mark.'

The men looked at him wonderingly and respectfully.

'You boys live here?' asked Rathburn.

'Sure,' was the reply. 'We work in the Pine Knot Hotel an' stables. You from the hills?'

'Yep,' answered Rathburn. 'Cow-puncher an' horseshoer an' one thing an' another. What's he doing now?' He again turned his attention to the scene within the resort, as did the two men with him.

The bandit was backing away from the bar toward the rear of the room, still keeping his guns thrust out before him, menacing the men who stood with uplifted hands.

'You can tell your funny judge that I called!' he sang out as he reached the rear door. 'An' now, gents,' he continued in an excited voice, 'it won't go well with the man that tries to get out this back way too soon.'

As he ceased speaking his guns roared. The two large hanging lamps, suspended from the ceiling in the center, went out to the accompaniment of shattered glass crashing on the floor. The three smaller lamps above the back bar next were cut to splinters by bullets and the place was in total darkness.

Then there was silence, save for the sound of a horse's hoofs coming from somewhere behind the building.

Rathburn drew back from the window as a match flared within and his two companions moved toward the front door. He stole around the corner of the building and started on a run for the rear. He stopped when he heard a horse galloping toward the east end of the street behind the buildings which lined that side. He hurried behind two buildings which did not extend as far as the resort and hastened up the street. He did not once look back.

Behind him he heard shouts and men running in the street. He increased his pace until he was running swiftly for the trees where he had left his horse. From above he caught the dying echoes of hoofs flying on the trail up the foothills by which he had come early that night.

The cries down the street increased, a gun barked, and bullets whined over his head.

'The locoed fools!' he panted. 'Didn't they hear that fellow ride away?'

But the shooting evidently was of a promiscuous nature, for he heard more shots around by the rear of the place where the robbery had been committed. No more bullets

30

were fired in his direction as he darted into the black shadows of the trees.

He quickly untied his horse, mounted, rode in the shelter of the timber to the east trail, and began the ascent, urging his horse to its fastest walking gait up the hard trail. The fleeing bandit's sounds of retreat no longer came to his ears, but he kept on, scanning the open stretches of trail above in the starlight, a disparaging smile playing upon his lips.

Back in the little town excitement was at a high pitch. Extra lamps had been lighted in the resort where a big crowd had gathered. Several men ran to the office of Judson Brown, justice of the peace, while others went in search of the constable.

When Brown failed to answer the summons at his door, some one discovered it was not locked, and the little group of men trooped in to find the justice gagged and handcuffed to his bed. They lighted the lamp and removed the gag. Then acting upon his instructions they took a bunch of keys from his pocket and unlocked the handcuffs.

He stood, boiling with rage, while they alternately hurled questions at him and told him of the holdup.

He ignored their questions as to how he came to be bound and gagged and demanded more details of the robbery.

'We took him to be The Coyote,' said the spokesman of the group. He had been one of the men the bandit had lined up. 'He was tall, an' blue or gray eyes, an'—'

'A puncher from up north picked him out through the window,' spoke up one of the men who had encountered Rathburn outside the resort. 'He'd been shot in the forearm by him once—showed us the scar. The robber was The Coyote, all right.'

'Certainly it was him!' roared Brown. 'He came in here, tied me up after pulling a gun on me, an' threatening to kill me, practically, so he wouldn't have any trouble pulling his trick. Tried to steer me off by saying he didn't come here to make any trouble. I knew he lied!'

The constable came in as the justice was finishing his irate speech.

'I'm going to lead this chase myself!' cried Brown. 'I want The Coyote, and I'm going to get him. I raise that reward to a thousand on the spot, and I know the sheriff will back me up. Get out every man in town that can stick on a horse, and we'll catch him if we have to comb the hills and desert country till doomsday!'

Already horsemen were gathering in the street outside. Feeling was high, for Dry Lake prided itself on its record of freedom from the molestation of outlaws. The rough element, too, was strong for a man hunt, or anything, for that matter, promising excitement.

A quarter of an hour later Brown, who was accepted as the leader when emergencies involving the law arose, distributed his forces. He sent two posses of twenty men each north and northwest. A third posse of a dozen men started southward. Towns to the west were notified by telephone as was the sheriff's office. The sheriff said he would be on his way to Dry Lake in an hour. He was amazed that The Coyote should be in his territory. He, too, wanted the outlaw, and he praised Brown for his reward offer.

Judson Brown himself led the posse of thirty men which took the east trail up the foothills. It was an hour past midnight. The moon had risen and was flooding the tumbled landscape with its cold, white light. From different vantage points on ridges high above, two men looked grimly down and saw the moving shadows of the man hunters as they took the trail.

CHAPTER FIVE

A CAPTURE

Three hours after the posses scattered on their search for The Coyote, spurred by thoughts of the reward of a thousand dollars offered by San Jacinto county, and Judson Brown's declaration that the reward would be increased by the thousands more which

Arizona had laid upon the fugitive's head, Rathburn smiled at the rosy dawn in supreme satisfaction.

He had not lost his man's trail during the early morning hours. Time and again he had outwitted the man ahead when the latter had waited to scan the back trail for signs of pursuit; more than once he had gained ground when screened by timber growth close to the trail; every stretch of dust-filled trail had been taken advantage of, while the soft going underfoot had deadened the sound of his horse's flying hoofs.

The bandit had traveled fast and he had kept steadily to the eastward. This last was what caused Rathburn to smile with satisfaction. The man for whose crime Rathburn was suspected was heading straight for Rathburn's own stamping ground—the far-distant desert range, which he knew from the low horizon in the south to the white-capped peaks in the north. To catch up with him would be but a matter of a few hours, Rathburn reflected contentedly.

Nor had the posse gained upon the two men ahead. Brown's men, perhaps, did not have as excellent specimens of horseflesh as Rathburn and his quarry rode. Nor did they possess the trail knowledge, the tricks which Rathburn knew, and which the latter, more or less to his surprise, found that the man ahead knew. Whatever it was that caused that curling,

34

sneering smile of contempt to play upon Rathburn's lips at intervals, it was not scorn of the riding ability of the man he was pursuing.

Moreover, both men ahead were saving their horses' strength against a probable spurt by the posse at daylight. It would not be a hard matter to follow their trail by the bright light of broad day. So far as he could determine, Rathburn did not believe the man ahead knew he was followed by a solitary rider who was between him and the hounds of the law.

Under the circumstances, the bandit would expect to be pursued by a number, Rathburn reasoned. He was ordering his pursuit on this theory, and he did not intend to take any more time than was absolutely necessary in catching up with the man ahead.

Rathburn's horse had not been hard ridden the day preceding, nor for several days before that. He had journeyed westward by easy stages, taking his time, favoring his mount in anticipation of some unforeseen emergency which might require hard riding. And he well knew the extraordinary powers of speed and endurance which the animal possessed.

He frowned as he thought of the brand. He had not been under the impression that the iron his horse wore was generally known to the authorities. He would have to hole-up somewhere in the hills before long and attend to that brand. As it was, it was a dead give-away as to his identity. He could thank Brown for this bit of information, anyway.

With the dawn, Rathburn found it easier to keep on his man's trail without being seen himself. He gained considerable until he estimated that he was not more than a mile and a half, or two miles at most, behind.

The sun was up when he reached the crest of the high ridge where was the tall pine and the sign which he had first seen the afternoon before.

He hesitated, debating whether to let the printed notice remain with his penciled inscription about the Arizona reward on it, or to tear it down. Then he saw the man he was pursuing below on the trail. He moved swiftly out of sight down the eastern side of the ridge. But when he came to the next vantage point he discovered that his man had apparently seen him; for he was riding at a mad gallop on the trail which wound eastward along the edge of the hills.

'Now's as good a time as any, hoss!' he cried to his mount as he drove in his spurs and dashed in swift pursuit.

Down the winding trail plunged horse and rider. The dun slipped and slid on the hard surface of the steep declivities and finally emerged upon the more open path which the man ahead was following.

Rathburn no longer made any attempt at concealment. He was after the man ahead, and, somewhere behind, a posse was in mad pursuit. If he were captured before he could overtake the bandit who was responsible for the robbery, the latter would very likely escape—was certain to make his getaway, in fact.

Rathburn called upon his horse by voice and spur for all the speed there was in him. He could see the fugitive ahead urging his horse to its utmost. The race was on in earnest. Thus they came to a long stretch of open, level trail. Here Rathburn's horse began slowly to gain.

The man ahead turned in his saddle, and Rathburn saw the glint of sunlight on dull metal. He brought out his own gun. But the other did not fire. He kept on, half-turned in the saddle, watching his pursuer keenly. Rathburn continued to gain upon him.

They now were less than half a mile apart, and the fugitive suddenly turned his horse due north, straight toward the hills, and sent a volley of shots whistling in his pursuer's direction.

Rathburn held his fire. The bullets flew wide of their mark, and he could see his man reloading as he rode. Rathburn now cut across, racing for the point where he thought the other would reach the hills. His horse rose to the emergency with a tremendous burst of speed. He was close enough now to shoot with a reasonable certainty of scoring a hit on his flying target. But he had no desire to kill, and he could not be certain, at that distance, of merely wounding his quarry. He also recoiled from the thought that he might accidentally hit the other's splendid horse.

Just ahead a thin line of straggling pines ranged down the gradual slope from the first low ridge of the hills for which they were heading. Rathburn swung north and gained the shelter of this screen just as the other rider again began firing. The trees now were between them, and each was an equal distance from the gentle slope of the ridge.

Rathburn called upon his horse for a last, heart-breaking burst of speed and the dun made good. At the beginning of the slope to the ridge, Rathburn veered sharply to the right and burst through the trees a scant rod or two from his man. His gun was leveled straight at the other, who had been caught momentarily off his guard.

'Drop it!' shouted Rathburn, racing toward him.

The man's right hand fell to his side while he checked his horse with his left. Rathburn rode in close to him and they came to a halt. Rathburn's lips were curled in a smile of contempt. The other stared at him, white-faced, his eyes wide and inquiring. The fingers of his right hand relaxed, and the gun fell to the ground. Rathburn swung low in the saddle and scooped it up, thrusting it into a pocket of his coat.

'Now beat it up over that ridge ahead,'

Rathburn ordered. 'And be quick about it. That posse may be close behind us.'

The other's eyes lit up with surprise. 'You—you're not an officer?' he stammered.

'Shut up, you fool!' cried Rathburn. 'You want to stay here an' talk when there's a score or two of men after us? I'm worse than an officer. Slope for that ridge now. Hurry!'

The man put the steel to his horse, and they dashed up the slope, crossed the ridge, and found themselves in a thick growth of timber which covered a large area.

'Pick your way into the middle of that patch of timber,' snapped out Rathburn. 'An' don't forget I'll be right close behind you. Get going—don't gape!'

The captive's face flushed at the other's manner and the indubitable note of contempt in his voice. But he obeyed the instructions and pushed into the timber.

When they had proceeded some distance Rathburn called a halt. 'Ever been in this country before?' he demanded with a sneer.

'Yes.' The other was more composed now. He studied his captor curiously and seemed more at ease. Evidently he was heartened by the fact that Rathburn had said he was not an officer and he believed him.

'I suppose you're after what I'm carrying on me,' he said with a touch of bitterness. 'I guess I'd have had as much chance as I've got now if I'd started shootin' even after you got the drop on me!'

Rathburn laughed harshly. 'You never had a chance from the start, if you only knew it,' he jeered. 'Why, you upstart, you're not entitled to any chance!'

The other man's face darkened in swift anger. 'Brave talk,' he said sneeringly. 'You've got me where you want me, so you can say anything.'

'I've got a pile to say,' replied Rathburn shortly. 'But this isn't the time or place to say it. We want to be good an' away out of that posse's path—an' quick.'

'You might as well take what you're after an' then each of us can look out for himself,' was the hot retort.

Rathburn looked at the man quizzically. 'You've got more spunk than I thought,' he mused.

He stared at the other man closely. The bandit could not have been more than twenty-five or twenty-six. He was tall, well-built, blond. His hair and eyes were about the color of Rathburn's. But Rathburn particularly noted the man's face, and whatever it was he saw there caused him to shrug and frown deeply.

'What's your name?' he demanded coldly.

'Percy,' sneeringly replied the other.

'That's good enough for me,' said Rathburn cheerfully. 'All I need is a name to call you by. Now, Percy, if you're acquainted with this country in here an' can steer the way to where the posse'll be liable to overlook us you better be leading on. I see you've ditched your other gun somewhere—you had two.'

'So you want me to take you where you'll be safe so you can rob me, maybe shoot me down, an' then make your getaway,' the other accused.

Rathburn looked him straight in the eyes. 'If you think I'm the kind of a man who'd shoot another down in cold blood when he was helpless you don't know much about human beings,' he said slowly. 'I have no intention of murdering you or harming you a-tall, if you're halfway careful. If you feel that it's against your principles to lead this expedition to temporary safety, we can turn back toward Dry Lake. We're going to do one thing or the other within one minute!'

'Oh, come on,' muttered the captive. He led the way through the timber to its western edge, then turned north in the shelter of the trees traversing a long, high, rocky ridge.

'Our horses won't leave any tracks here,' he called back. 'Or maybe you don't care whether we leave any tracks or not,' he added sarcastically.

Rathburn spurred his horse alongside of him. 'It doesn't make a bit of difference to me,' he said. 'You're the one that's got to be scared of that posse, Percy, not me. If it wasn't for one thing I'd take you right down there to

41

meet 'em!'

The other looked at him both in anger and perplexity. 'Suppose you'd object to tellin' what that one thing is,' he said savagely.

'Well, it may be that I feel sorry for you,' said Rathburn as if to himself. 'An' it may be that I want credit for bringing you in without the help of any posse an' without them knowing it!'

CHAPTER SIX

THE REAL LOW-DOWN

They rode on in silence. When they reached the north end of the ridge the man in the lead turned west on a slope studded with large boulders and rock outcroppings. There was considerable shale here, too, and they had to proceed cautiously in spots, both for fear of sliding down the shale and to prevent making much noise.

'If they follow us up here, we can hear 'em before they get to us,' said the man who called himself Percy, with a shrug and a frowning look at his companion.

Rathburn did not reply.

They continued across the slope and descended into a large bowl or pocket, guarded by huge boulders and scattering trees on the slope above.

'Guess it's safe to rest our horses here,' said Percy. 'We can hear 'em coming either way; but I don't think they'll get up here.'

However, neither he nor Rathburn knew how many men Brown had at his command, nor did they know that the sheriff of the county, with two deputies, had raced to Dry Lake by automobile, procured horses, and hastened to join Brown on the east trail, which seemed the most likely route of escape for the outlaw.

There was a spring in the pocket surrounded by a small meadow of good grass. The pair watered their horses, loosened their saddle-cinches, and permitted the animals to graze with reins dangling.

Rathburn took his slicker pack from the rear of his saddle and spread it open on the ground.

'Reckon it's safe to build a small fire here?' he asked cheerfully. 'I'm powerful hungry, an' I've got some emergency provisions—being trail-broke.'

Percy, too, was hungry, as his eager look toward the pack testified.

'I'll climb up to the top on the lower side an' keep an eye out while you fix some grub,' he volunteered. 'You needn't be scared of me jumping over the other side. There's a drop of about five hundred feet over there.'

'Go ahead and jump if you want,' said

Rathburn. 'Me—I'd rather live. That's why I want to eat.'

While the other climbed to his lookout position Rathburn made a fire. Then he took a small frying pan and coffeepot, minus its handle, from the pack, removed the packages stuffed in them, and soon was making coffee, frying bacon, and warming up beans. This, with some hard biscuits and some sirup out of a bottle, constituted their meal, which Rathburn soon had ready.

Again he looked closely at Percy's face as the latter scrambled down from his perch to appease his hunger.

Suddenly he burst out laughing; but it was a belittling laugh, half sneering, which brought the blood to the face of the captive while Rathburn watched him closely.

'If I had today's actions to do over again you mightn't be so tickled,' said the man viciously.

'I'm laughing to think how lucky you are for a rank beginner an' botcher!' said Rathburn as they began to eat. 'You must have took a course in outlawing from some correspondence school,' he continued.

'Maybe you could have done better,' hinted the other.

'Quite likely I could,' admitted Rathburn. 'In the first place I'd have shut that back door after I came in so nobody could pot shot me from behind. Yes, I reckon I'd have done that.'

Percy glared at him thoughtfully.

'Then I wouldn't have let myself get in line with the front and side windows,' Rathburn taunted. 'Lots of men are shot through windows. Ever hear of such a thing?'

His listener didn't answer.

'An' now that I think of it,' Rathburn droned on, 'I'd have lined those men up against the wall with their faces turned *away* from me. That puts 'em at more of a disadvantage, an' they can't see what's going on.'

Percy now was regarding him keenly.

'Let's see,' said Rathburn, with tantalizing slowness. 'Oh, yes, Percy. I wouldn't have taken anything from the cash drawers but the bills. I don't like to take the time to monkey around with a lot of silver; besides, it sort of weights one down.'

He paused long enough to let that sink in, then continued: 'The thing I'd have paid most of my attention to—excepting for keeping a watchful eye on the men against the wall an' the windows an' doors—would have been the safe. The big money's usually in the safe, an' the bartender can be induced to open the safe just as easy as he can be persuaded into opening the cash drawers. An' say, Percy, I'd never let a bartender get as close to me as you let that fellow get to you. He might start something, then you'd have to begin shootin' an' that would alarm the town an' ball up the program.'

'You talk like you'd had considerable

experience,' observed Percy warily.

'Maybe so. Maybe I have. But if I have, I can say I've never pulled anything quite so raw as the way you pulled that stunt last night down in Dry Lake, Percy. That is the real low-down on that. You just naturally laid yourself open to attack from all quarters.'

His captive looked at him both respectfully and sheepishly.

'An' there's only one reason why you got away with it,' said Rathburn, his eyes narrowing.

'Because I was lucky like you say, I suppose,' sneeringly answered Percy.

'No!' thundered Rathburn. 'You got away with it because they thought you were The Coyote!'

The captive started; stared at Rathburn with widened eyes.

'That's why you got away with it,' continued Rathburn in a hard voice. 'An' you thought you'd cinch it when you told 'em before you went out that they could tell their funny judge you called!'

Rathburn's eyes blazed with angry contempt. 'Trading on somebody else's name,' he mocked. 'Trying to make out you was the goods, an' I believe they thought you was The Coyote, at that. Man, I saw the whole dirty business.'

Percy's face went white. However, his emotion was more anger than fear, and he was prey to an overpowering curiosity.

'How do you know I *ain't* The Coyote?' he asked shrewdly.

Rathburn stared at him—stunned. Then he leaped to his feet and his gun flashed into his hand in a movement too swift for the eye to follow.

'Go over there and look at the brand on my horse,' he commanded. 'Remember how that printed bill read that put it in your fool head to try an' masquerade as The Coyote, an' then read the brand on that horse!'

The captive rose and without a look back walked to where Rathburn's horse was cropping the grass. The left side of the animal was toward him and for a few moments he stood looking with bulging eyes at the CC2 on the shoulder. Then he turned slowly.

Rathburn's gaze burned into his, but a cool, deliberate light had come into his eyes.

'So you're The Coyote!' Percy said quietly. 'I should have recognized you.'

'Yes, I'm called The Coyote,' said Rathburn, walking slowly toward him. 'I'm the man they think robbed that joint down in Dry Lake last night. I'm the man they're looking for. I'm the man they want to make pay for your bungling work. That's the way it's gone for three years, Percy. I've been blamed for job after job that I didn't even know was pulled off till I heard they were looking for me on account of it. But this is one job they'll not be able to lay at my

47

door; for I've got the man who's responsible an' I've got him red-handed!'

'What're you going to do about it?' asked the other coolly.

Again Rathburn's eyes blazed with rage. 'Do? Why, I'm just naturally going to take you in all by my lonesome an' turn you over to the sheriff with my compliments.'

Rathburn cooled down as he said this, drew tobacco and papers from his shirt pocket, and proceeded to build a cigarette. He looked at his man queerly.

'Now I reckon you know why I ain't got any idea of taking that money off you,' he said.

'They might not believe you,' returned the other.

'I know what you mean. You mean they might think I was putting up a job on 'em an' trying to shift the blame on somebody else. It can't be done, Percy. Listen to this: I was looking through the front window of that place last night when you held it up. Two men that work in the hotel down there came along an' looked in alongside of me after I warned 'em not to go in. I showed 'em this scar on my arm.' He rolled back his left sleeve disclosing a scar on the forearm about three inches below the elbow.

'I told 'em that scar was made by a bullet from The Coyote's gun,' Rathburn went on, pulling down his sleeve and drawing his right hand back to the gun he had replaced in its holster. 'That scar *was* made by The Coyote's gun. I shot myself in the arm by accident some few years ago. Now, here's the point: Those men will remember me an' remember that scar. The descriptions the sheriff of that county must have in his office will tell all about that scar. It won't be hard to identify me by it an' by the two men that stood out there by the window with me. So they'll know I didn't pull the robbery!'

The other man shifted uneasily on his feet.

'An' that ain't all, Percy,' Rathburn continued. 'Somebody saw me running up the street afterward because they took a couple of shots at me for luck. That'll dovetail with my story. I've never been known to use two guns. An' if they want any more proof all they'll have to do will be to stand you up in front of the men you had in line, dressed as you are with that black handkerchief over your face. That'll settle it. I reckon the sheriff will believe me an' give me a chance when he hears the facts, or I may not wait for a talk with him.'

'I take it you've got me right,' said the captive, compressing his lips. 'But if you're really The Coyote I've heard so much about, you'll give me my gun an' give me a chance to run for it!'

Rathburn's laugh jarred on his ears. 'Give you a chance an' take a chance myself on going to the gallows?'

'The gallows!' exclaimed the other. 'Oh—I

49

see. But didn't you say you thought the sheriff would give you a chance if he met you an' heard your story? At that you don't have to stay around an' get taken back to Arizona now.'

'They hang men in this State,' Rathburn interrupted.

'But—there wasn't—' The other man faltered, staring.

'One of those shots you fired at the lamp went wild, or glanced off something, an'—' Rathburn lifted his brows significantly.

'Killed somebody!' cried the other.

He staggered back just as a rattle of falling stones signified that horsemen were in the shale on the slope to eastward.

CHAPTER SEVEN

WHERE TO HIDE

For the space of several seconds Rathburn and his captive looked into each other's eyes. Rathburn's gaze was keen, alert, fired by the quick thinking he was doing. Stark terror showed in the other's look which gradually changed to one of haunting fear and indecision. Then his eyes became clear and he returned Rathburn's glance, cool and questioning.

'Get your horse,' ordered Rathburn, running to his own mount.

In a twinkling he had tightened his cinch, caught up the reins, and vaulted into the saddle. His captive was at his side shortly afterward.

'You're still in the lead,' Rathburn snapped out; 'unless you want to wait for 'em.'

The other whirled his horse, sent him flying for the western end of the pocket, with Rathburn close behind. They went up a steep, rocky trail, screened by boulders. When they reached the top of the west rim they looked back and saw four horsemen on the shale slope leading to the pocket. Brown evidently had split up his posse and was literally combing the hills for his quarry.

'They'll know they're on the right trail when they see the remains of our dinner an' my pack down there,' remarked Rathburn dryly.

'But they haven't seen us yet,' said Percy breathlessly. 'If we can make Sunrise Cañon Trail we can lose 'em in the mountains—that is if *you* want to lose 'em.'

'Where's the trail?' asked Rathburn.

' 'Bout five miles west. It's the only trail goin' up into the big mountains between here an' the other side of the Dry Lake range, an' it's a tough one.'

Rathburn quickly sized up the country ahead. He saw low and high ridges with towering mountains to the right, or north, of them. There were scattering pines on the slopes and patches of timber in the wide ravines, many of which were veritable valleys.

'We'll run for it while they're getting in an' out of that hole,' he suddenly decided with a click of his teeth. 'Their horses are in no better shape than ours. Slope along.'

The other had dug in his spurs even before he got the order. They rode swiftly down the steep trail from the rim of the pocket and fled across an open space and up the slope of the first ridge.

Rathburn looked back as they crossed it, but could see no sign of their pursuers. His face still was troubled; his gaze kept boring into the back of the man on the horse ahead of him. At times he muttered to himself.

They galloped up the hard bed of a dry arroyo and swung westward across another rock-bound ridge, picking their way carefully among the boulders. Rathburn's face became more and more strained as he noted that the leader evidently knew the country they were in like a book. Rathburn, with the experience born of years spent in the open places, was able to keep his bearings.

They had followed a course for some miles north of the main trail leading east, the trail by which he had first come into the locality. Then they had doubled back westward, some miles above that trail, of course, and now were heading almost due north again, in the direction of the mountains which did not appear to be far away. He surmised that they were nearly directly north of the ranch where he had had the meal with the girl and boy.

At the top of the next ridge his guide pointed above them.

'See that crack in the mountain?' he said.

Rathburn nodded as he made out what appeared to be a gash in the steep side of a mountain north of them.

'That's Sunrise Cañon,' said the other quietly. 'There's a trail up that cañon into the heart of the mountains where they couldn't catch us—or you, if you want to go alone—in a hundred years!'

He stared steadily at Rathburn.

'Mosey along, then,' said Rathburn. 'Let's get somewhere's before our horses drop.'

They kept along the ridge until it was cut by a cañon. Here they descended and entered another long, narrow ravine which they negotiated at a gallop. At its upper end they again climbed a steep slope. Their horses were showing the strain of the hours of hard riding. Rathburn realized that they could go but a limited distance. But the members of the posse most assuredly must be in the same fix so far as their mounts were concerned.

He decided that if they could get into the cañon unseen they would be able to rest their horses and remain secure for the night. Next morning they could continue on up into the hills, or slip back by a roundabout way to Dry Lake.

His lips froze into a thin white line. He did not look at the man with him as they paused for a few moments under the trees which covered the top of the ridge and gazed at a long, gently sloping stretch of nearly open country. It was covered with clumps of trees at intervals, that reached to the dark, narrow opening in the mountains, marking the entrance to Sunrise Cañon and the trail to the fastnesses of the higher hills.

'You can swing off here to the left an' down a wide valley to where there's a cut-off into Dry Lake,' he heard his captive suggesting. 'I don't see any sense in all this hard ridin' an' hidin' if you're goin' to turn me in.'

'We'll go on,' growlingly replied Rathburn.

They descended the ridge and entered the long, sloping valley, so wide that it virtually was a plain. They made good headway, although they favored their horses. They took advantage of the shelter provided by the occasional clumps of pines. The afternoon was drawing to a close with the sun dipping sharply toward the western hills when they came in sight of the entrance to the cañon. But with the first glimpse they checked their horses and turned into the shelter of some trees near by.

'Beat us to it!' exclaimed Percy.

'Four of 'em,' said Rathburn, frowning. 'Brown ain't taking any chances. He's a better

54

man than I figured him out. An' there's more of 'em!'

He pointed westward where two riders were barely discernible on the crest of a ridge. They disappeared almost immediately in the timber below.

'We'll turn back,' Rathburn decided. 'We'll ride with the trees between us an' the men up at the cañon, an' keep an eye out for the pair to the west. You might watch that side, an' I'll look out for the east an' south. C'mon, let's drift.'

The face of the man who called himself Percy was white and strained as they urged their tired mounts southward. They skirted the western end of the ridge by which they had gained the wide valley and continued on, carefully scanning the landscape in all directions for indications of pursuit. It was plain to them that they had been seen to leave the east trail early that morning. Brown and his men undoubtedly knew they had headed north, and the justice had immediately dispatched men to guard the entrance to the cañon trail into the mountains. Then they had begun a systematic search of the locality.

This deduction was strengthened when Rathburn suddenly pointed toward the east. More riders were to be seen on the slope of the valley's side in that direction. Even as they looked, these riders, too, disappeared from view as they dropped down behind a rise of ground.

The sun was going down fast. Already the red banners of the sunset were flaunted in the high western skies. The twilight would be upon them apace—the long-lasting, purple-veiled twilight of the altitudes. Then the night would close down with its canopy of stars.

Rathburn looked speculatively at his companion. 'We'll make a break for that clump of trees about a quarter of a mile ahead with all our horses have got left,' he said, driving in his spurs.

In a last mad dash which taxed every iota of strength and endurance left in their beasts they gained the shelter of the little patch of timber.

'Here we'll wait,' said Rathburn coolly as he dismounted.

'What?' cried the other, staring at him incredulously. 'We ain't quite surrounded yet. We haven't seen anybody in the south. That way may be open an' it's liable to be closed while we're stayin' here.'

'Get off your horse and unsaddle him,' commanded Rathburn sternly. 'The best place to hide from a posse is in the middle of it!'

CHAPTER EIGHT

TWO QUEER MOVES

The captive complied with the order, looking at Rathburn in a peculiar way—half disgusted, half contemptuous. Indeed, he turned his back on the other, leaned against the slender trunk of a pine, and stared steadily into the south. He appeared much worried.

The horses welcomed the chance to rest.

Rathburn walked slowly back and forth the width of the patch of timber, vigilantly keeping watch. He paid no attention whatsoever to the man leaning against the tree. For all the interest he displayed he might have completely forgotten his very existence. In time this got on the other's nerves.

'I believe you lied when you said there was a man killed down there last night,' he said coolly.

'I didn't say anybody was killed,' Rathburn returned without looking in his direction. 'You assumed that part of it.'

'Then you wanted me to think so,' said the other in a loud voice. 'You was tryin' to throw a scare into me!'

Rathburn swung on his heel and stepped squarely in front of him. 'I let you think that to show you what *might* have happened,' he said.

'Such things have happened to me an' swelled the price on my head. Now, darn you, if you talk that loud again I'll choke your wind off!'

The words came with sinister earnestness, but they seemed to rouse some dormant strain of extraordinary courage in the man to whom they were addressed.

He suddenly leaped from the tree and struck out with all the force at his command.

But Rathburn had anticipated the attack. He knocked the other's blow aside and drove his right straight to the jaw.

'There's a little souvenir to show you that I mean business, Percy,' he panted.

Percy came back to the attack with eyes gleaming with malice. Again he attempted to hit Rathburn, but the latter stepped aside with lightning swiftness and drove home another blow. He followed it up with a left and right and Percy sprawled his length on the grass.

After a time he sat up, dazed. Rathburn was standing over him. But although he realized fully that he was not a match for Rathburn in physical combat, and doubtless was greatly his inferior with his gun, his spirit was undaunted.

'You better finish me, or drag me in,' he gritted; 'for I'll get you, if I can. I don't know what your play is, but you've acted too queer today for me to believe you're on the square one way or the other.'

'You want some more, Percy?'

'My name is Lamy,' growlingly replied the

other, as he rose cautiously.

'Oh, o-h. Percy Lamy.'

'No, just Lamy. Lamy's my name, an' I ain't ashamed of it. You'd find it out—sooner or later—anyway, I—expect.' He stammered during this speech as if he had just remembered something—remembered when it was too late.

Rathburn noted the frown and the confused expression in Lamy's eyes. He turned abruptly and walked away.

A few minutes later he came back to find Lamy sitting with his back to a tree, staring unseeing into the deepening twilight.

'Lamy,' he said harshly, 'we're going to get away from this posse—maybe. Anyway, soon's it's dark we'll ride south. It's just possible we can leave 'em up here in the hills.'

'Suppose I refuse to go?'

'Then I'll have to truss you up an' tie you to your horse, an' don't think I won't do it!' The ring of menace in Rathburn's voice convinced the other, but he made no comment.

When darkness had fallen they saddled their mounts and started. They rode at a jog, keeping as much as possible in the shadow of the timber. Rathburn noticed that the valley gradually widened; he showed interest in his surroundings.

Then, off to the left below them, he saw moving shadows. He called a halt at the next clump of trees. 'Lamy, are there any horses running in here that you know of?' he asked.

'There probably are,' said Lamy sarcastically; 'an' they've probably got riders on 'em.'

'No doubt,' returned Rathburn gravely. 'I just saw some shadows that looked like horses down to the left of us.'

'I expected they'd shut us off in the south,' snapped out Lamy. 'You gave 'em plenty of time.'

'We just naturally had to rest our horses,' observed Rathburn. 'As it is, they're not good for far, nor for any fast riding. Besides, I've changed my mind some since this morning.'

'So? I suppose you're goin' to give me a chance?' sneeringly inquired the other.

He could see Rathburn's eyes in the twilight, and suddenly he shifted in his saddle uneasily. For Rathburn's gaze had narrowed; and it shot from his eyes steel blue with a flash of fire. His face had set in cold, grim lines. The whole nature of the man seemed to undergo a change. He radiated menace, contempt, cold resentment. The corners of his mouth twisted down sharply. His voice, as he spoke now, seemed edged like a knife.

'Lamy, hand over that money!'

Lamy's brows lifted in swift comprehension; a look of cunning came into his eyes—was followed by a gleam of hope, not unmixed with derision. He thrust his hands into his coat pockets and held out bills and silver to

Rathburn who stuffed the plunder into his own pockets.

'That all of it?' demanded Rathburn sharply. He made no effort to temper the tones of his voice.

For answer Lamy dug into his trousers' pockets, under his chaps, and produced two more rolls of bills.

'That's the chunk,' he said with a sneering inflection in his voice. 'If you want I'll stand a frisk.'

'No, I won't search you. I take it you're too sensible to lie!'

'Thanks,' replied Lamy dryly. 'I suppose I'm free to go now, unless you figure you'd be safer by killin' me off.'

Anger, swift and uncontrollable, leaped into Rathburn's eyes. Then he laughed, softly and mirthlessly. 'If I'd been minded to do for you, or had any such idea in my head, I'd have given it to you long before this,' he said. 'It's lucky for you, Lamy, that I'm pretty much the breed you thought I was.'

'Don't pose!' retorted Lamy hotly. 'You intended to get that money and make me the goat if you could, from the start. If you'd had any idea of turnin' me over to Brown you'd have done that little thing, too, long before this.'

'Maybe so,' Rathburn mused, staring at the other thoughtfully in the dim light of the stars. 'Maybe I will yet. You're not out of this—an'

61

neither am I. Those shadows down to the left are getting plainer. What's that long dark streak over there on the right?'

'Those are trees,' answered Lamy sneeringly.

'Let's make for 'em,' ordered Rathburn. 'Don't forget you're still under orders, Lamy. An' don't overlook the fact that I'm more or less in earnest about things in general,' he added significantly.

They rode at a tangent for the dark shadow of the trees. At the edge of the timber ensued another long wait, with Rathburn uncommunicative, moodily pacing restlessly back and forth. The horses had another excellent opportunity to rest and the fagged animals took advantage of it.

Once or twice Rathburn thought he glimpsed a light far down the valley, but he couldn't be sure. Neither could he be sure he saw the moving shadows on the opposite side of the wide valley again.

The night wore into early morning and the moon added its cold radiance to the faint glow of the myriads of stars. Rathburn sensed the nearness of enemies. Several times he stopped before Lamy, who sat upon his saddle blanket with his back against a tree trunk and dozed. Rathburn had to fight off continual drowsiness.

For long hours he walked along the edge of the pines. He dared not trust himself to sleep.

He dared not trust Lamy to stand guard while he obtained some rest, and he knew that when the sun came up and the day began, he would be thoroughly awake again; for more than once he had gone two nights without sleep. Also, he assumed that the hunt would be less spirited during the night. Members of the posse would themselves be drowsy, but they could spell each other and in that way maintain their vigil and secure a few hours of rest.

Rathburn's rage rose at frequent intervals as he thought of the predicament he was in through no fault of his own. More than once he glared malevolently at the sleeping Lamy; then the troubled look would come again to his eyes and he would resume his pacing, muttering to himself, staring into the blue veil of the night. Once he sat down and removed his right boot and sock in the darkness; shortly afterward he again began his pacing.

He felt the pangs of hunger and shook his head savagely as he thought of the scanty supply of provisions he had been compelled to leave in the mountain pocket.

His spirits revived as he thought of the horses. They would be fresh in the morning; and he intended that his horse should have a grain feed that day. Rathburn always thought of his horse first; and, although it might seem that he taxed the animal's powers to their utmost at times, he never went beyond a certain point. He had often said he would surrender to his pursuers rather than kill his mount in evading them.

The first faint glimmer of the dawn was lighting the skies above the ridges to the eastward when he roused Lamy. He awoke with a start, stared sleepily at Rathburn, then got speedily to his feet.

'You been awake all night?' he asked curiously.

Rathburn nodded, looking at him closely. 'Saddle up,' he ordered.

They rode southward at a canter in the shelter of the edge of the timber. When the eastern skies were rosy red and fast changing to gold with the advent of the sun they saw two things; a small ranch house about a mile southeast of them, and two riders some distance north.

Rathburn reined in his mount. He looked at Lamy who met his gaze in defiance. Then Rathburn reached into his coat pocket with his right hand and drew out a gun.

'Here's your shooting iron,' he said, as he held the weapon out to Lamy.

The other stared at him in astonishment.

'Take it!' snapped out Rathburn. 'Take it, or I may change my mind!'

Lamy took the gun wonderingly, balanced it for a moment in his hand, and shoved it into his holster.

Rathburn motioned toward the south and

Lamy rode along at his side. They caught another glimpse of the horsemen in the north. As they drew opposite the ranch house, on the west or front side, they saw a woman leave it and walk the short distance to the barn and enter. At that moment both Rathburn and Lamy gave vent to low exclamations. They had caught sight of riders in the south and to the east. They appeared to be surrounded by the posse.

Rathburn looked at Lamy soberly. However, it was Lamy who spoke first. 'You said the best place to hide from a posse was in the middle of it,' he said scornfully. 'Why not leave the horses in the timber an' run for the house? Maybe it has a cellar.'

'I reckon that would he as good a move as any,' replied Rathburn, to the other's surprise. 'I'm game if you are.'

Lamy's eyes flamed with excitement as he turned his mount into the trees. They came to what looked like a bear pit or a prospect hole. It was partly filled with brush.

'We can hide our saddles in there an' let the horses go,' Lamy suggested. 'There's a few horses runnin' in through here, an' they may join 'em.'

'You can do that with yours,' said Rathburn grimly. 'You seem to forget that the brand on this dun is pretty well known.'

He coolly tied his horse as Lamy followed his own suggestion, hid his saddle, and turned his mount loose.

They moved back to the edge of the timber and waited until they could see no one in sight about the house or in any direction in the valley. Then they started on a run for the house.

CHAPTER NINE

LEAVE IT TO ME

Rathburn had recognized the ranch long before they came close to it. It was the place where he had stopped for a meal with the girl and the freckle-faced boy two days before— the day he had gone on into Dry Lake. He saw no sign of the girl or the boy or any one else as they reached the front door and hurried inside.

Out of the corner of his eye he saw Lamy look hurriedly about and step into the kitchen. He followed him.

Lamy grabbed part of a loaf of bread and some cold meat on a shelf above the kitchen table.

'There's usually a cellar under the main room in these square houses,' he said, hurrying back into the larger room.

Rathburn stepped after him, and Lamy pulled back the rug before the table and disclosed a trapdoor. He raised the door, held out the food to Rathburn, and whispered: 'You better get down there. Take this grub an'—'

'What's the matter? Isn't there room for both of us?' Rathburn put the question in a voice which conveyed surprise.

'I thought it might be better if we—if we didn't both hide in the same place,' whispered Lamy. 'Then they'd only get one of us, an' whichever it was they'd think he was the one they wanted, see?' He appeared excited.

Rathburn's eyes narrowed. His right hand darted to his gun in a flash, and the muzzle of the weapon was pressed into Lamy's ribs. 'Get down there!' commanded Rathburn. 'Get down.'

Lamy hesitated with a wild look in his eyes. The muzzle of Rathburn's gun pressed harder against his midriff. He dropped lightly into the cellar. Rathburn pulled the rug against the trapdoor as he followed, then let down the door, certain that the rug would fall into place.

The pair sat upon some gunny sacks in the little cellar until their eyes became accustomed to the darkness; they could dimly see each other by the faint light which came to them through some cracks in the floor above.

They heard steps at the rear of the house; then the pound of hoofs from in front. Rathburn saw Lamy staring at him fixedly with a puzzled look. He frowned at him. Rathburn still held his gun in his hand. Both had forgotten the food which Lamy had in his lap.

'Say,' whispered Lamy. 'What was your idea in givin' me back my gun?'

He moved closer to get the reply.

'Shut up!' said Rathburn, cocking an ear toward the trapdoor.

The sound of footsteps now was in the kitchen. They heard horses snorting and men dismounting at the front door. After a brief space there were light foot-steps in the room above followed by the tramp of heavy boots.

'Good morning, ma'am,' came a deep voice.

'Good morning,' was the hesitating reply. Rathburn recognized the voice of the girl who had fed him.

'Ma'am, I'm Sheriff Neal of San Jacinto County,' continued the deep voice, as several feet shuffled slightly. 'These men with me are members of my posse. Maybe you know Judge Brown?'

'I—I've seen him,' answered the girl.

Rathburn could feel Lamy's knees shaking against him in excitement.

'I believe we've met some time,' Brown put in. Rathburn thought the justice's voice sounded tired.

'Ma'am, we're looking for a man—or two men.' It was the sheriff speaking again. 'Have you seen anyone around here this morning— any stranger, or strangers, I mean?'

'Why, no,' replied the girl with a breathless catch in her voice. 'I haven't seen any one.'

'You're sure?'

Rathburn frowned at the sheriff's tone, although he kept his eyes on Lamy's white face.

He smiled as he remembered that the sheriff had mentioned two men. This doubtless was the cause of Lamy's agitation. Nor did he think Lamy had forgotten that he, Rathburn, had pointed out that he could prove he didn't rob the place in Dry Lake.

'You're sure?' the sheriff asked again.

'Why yes,' replied the girl. 'I am sure.'

'Maybe she can get us some breakfast,' said Brown hopefully.

'Can you feed five men, ma'am?' asked the sheriff in a softer tone.

'Just sit down, and I'll get you some breakfast,' said the girl.

The two men in the little cellar could hear some of the men taking chairs and one or two going out to look after the horses. The girl's light footsteps retreated into the kitchen.

Rathburn smiled mysteriously at Lamy who was shivering with a case of nerves.

'I can't understand who that was with him—or following him,' came Brown's voice. 'Somebody must have seen him getting away and set out on the trail while it was hot.'

'Either that or saw him beating it somewheres on the trail east of town an' took after him on suspicion,' drawled the sheriff. ' 'Spect everybody around here has seen those reward notices you put out.'

'That's so,' said Brown. 'I had the right hunch when I got the tip he'd left his Arizona hangout, sheriff. I figured he'd head this way. Then he had the nerve—well, you know what happened in my office.'

The sheriff chuckled. Then he spoke angrily. 'He can't pull any of his stunts in my territory,' he said growlingly. 'I'll hunt him down if I have to put every man I've got on the trail an' keep 'em there. I figure, though,' he added hopefully, 'that we've got him cornered in or around this valley. We traced 'em here, and we got sight of 'em yesterday. We'll have 'em before night!'

'I hope so,' said Brown grimly.

'I've given orders to shoot to kill and not to miss,' thundered the sheriff. 'But I guess the rewards offered for him would kind of steady the aim of the man that got a crack at him.'

Rathburn's face went white, and his eyes shot fire as he listened to the sheriff's cruel laugh in which the others in the room above now joined.

Lamy signaled that he wished to whisper in his ear, and Rathburn bent his head, although he kept the gun handy.

'I'm not goin' to risk shootin' anybody if we should be found or cornered,' Lamy whispered. 'I thought you ought to know—'

'If we're cornered you leave it to me,' Rathburn came back. 'I have reasons for everything I'm doing. An' don't forget that I'd rather be grabbed for this simple trick of yours in Dry Lake than for one or two jobs over in Arizona. If things go wrong keep your mouth shut—don't talk! If you start talking any time I'll try to kill you!'

Lamy drew back from the ferocity in Rathburn's tone and manner. That menacing message was again in Rathburn's eyes.

'Who's that boy out there?' the sheriff called sharply.

'Go in and say how-do-you-do,' came the girl's voice from the kitchen. 'It's my brother, Frankie.'

'Come here, Frankie,' said the sheriff.

The pair below heard light footsteps on the floor above.

'That's a fine crop of freckles you've got,' said the sheriff.

Rathburn saw Lamy put a hand to his face and make a grimace.

'Listen, Frankie, did you see anybody around here this morning?' asked the sheriff.

'Who—who you looking for?' asked the boy. Rathburn started; his body suddenly tensed. 'I'm looking for an outlaw they call The Coyote,' returned the sheriff. 'Ever hear of him?'

'Y-e-s. Ed brought home a notice about a reward for him.'

'That's the man we're after. Rides a dun-colored horse; tall, light-complexioned. Seen anybody like that around here.'

'He was here day before yesterday,' said the boy truthfully. 'Sis gave him something to eat, an' he went on into town. He didn't seem like such a bad man to me. Told me never to lie.'

'He was here? Ate here?' The sheriff's voice was excited.

Rathburn saw Lamy's eyes widen.

'Frankie,' the sheriff said soberly, 'that Coyote went into town an' robbed a place. He's a bad, dangerous man no matter how he looks or what he says. Have you seen anybody that looked like him since?'

The question was followed by a deep silence. Rathburn alert, his eyes gleaming, heard the sheriff rise.

'Answer me, boy. I'm the sheriff of this county!'

' 'Tain't that—'tain't that,' said the boy in a tremulous voice. 'Only—I'd rather not tell, Mr. Sheriff.'

'You must answer me!' said the official sternly. 'Have you seen any one around here— yesterday or this morning?'

'Ye-e-s.'

'When?' demanded the sheriff. 'Don't lie!'

'This—this morning,' stammered the boy.

'Where? Tell me about it, quick.'

'Two men ran across from the timber to the house,' replied the boy. 'He—he said not to lie for him—but—'

The sheriff stepped quickly to the kitchen door. 'I thought you said no one had been

72

around here, ma'am.'

'Why—I didn't see any one,' came the girl's voice.

'I saw 'em from the pasture,' the boy confessed.

'Then they're here!' cried the sheriff. 'Search the house an' the barn!'

In the dim, narrow cellar Rathburn was holding his gun aimed at Lamy's heart.

'You remember what I said about keepin' your mouth shut?' he asked in a low voice, his steel-blue gaze boring into the other's eyes.

Lamy gasped. Then he slowly nodded his head.

'That's your bond!' said Rathburn, as tramping feet sounded overhead.

CHAPTER TEN

CAUGHT IN THE CELLAR

Rathburn rose and crouched under the trapdoor, gun in hand. Lamy watched him, breathless, perplexed, uncertain. They heard men running; then there were no sounds from above and a deathly stillness settled down.

Slowly and with infinite care Rathburn raised the trapdoor an inch or two and listened intently. Lamy scrambled to his knees on the pile of gunny sacks; but Rathburn swung quickly upon him. They stared at each other in the semidarkness.

'He said two,' breathed Lamy, a curious look in his eyes.

'Are you afraid?' mocked Rathburn. 'It's me they want—don't worry. I may make a break for it, an' if I do there's likely to be powder burned. You can stay here an' get out when they take after me, if I go,' said Rathburn, and the sneer in his voice caused Lamy to flush uncomfortably.

Rathburn petted the gun in his hand. 'But before I make a break I want to tell you something that I should have told you before this, when I had more time—'

He bit off his speech as there came a sudden recurrence of the sounds in the house. The trapdoor closed down.

'Where's the cellar?' came the sheriff's authoritative voice.

Many feet tramped upon the floor above them. Then they heard the rug stripped back. There was an exclamation from the sheriff and the sound of moving feet suddenly was stilled.

'Is there any one in the cellar?' the sheriff called.

Silence—with Lamy pressing Rathburn's knee with a hand, and Rathburn smiling that queer, grim smile which conveyed so much, yet nothing which was tangible.

'Get around here, you fellows,' they heard the sheriff order.

The sound of boots and spurs attested to the quickness with which his order was obeyed.

Rathburn leaned down suddenly and with lightning swiftness jerked Lamy's gun from its holster near his side. He tossed the weapon to a corner of the dark cellar just as the sheriff's voice was heard again.

'Coyote, if you're down there I'm not going to take a chance fumbling with that door. If you ain't there, then there won't be any harm in what I'm going to do. If I don't hear anything when I finish talking I'm going to give the signal to my men to start shooting through the floor—and I mean it. If anybody's down there it'd be good sense to flip up that door and crawl out hands first, an' those hands empty.'

'Sheriff, you're bluffing!' said Rathburn loudly.

Then the sheriff spoke again in an exultant tone. 'I figured it was the best hidin' place you could find, Coyote. You're right; I was sort of bluffing, but I might have changed my mind an' gone on through with it. We've got you dead to rights, Coyote; you haven't got a chance. There's seven of us now an' every man is ready to open up if you come out of there a-shooting.'

Rathburn slipped his gun back into his holster. He raised the trapdoor slowly until it tipped back on the floor leaving the opening into the cellar clear.

'Two of 'em!' he heard some one exclaim.

He looked up to accustom his eyes to the light and saw a dozen guns covering him.

'Gentlemen, the landscape fairly bristles with artillery,' he said amiably. 'Who's the sheriff? And—there's Jud Brown. Who let you loose, Jud?'

'I'm Sheriff Neal,' interposed that individual, a slight, dark man with a bristly mustache. 'Come out of there—hands free.'

'For the time being, eh, sheriff? I expect you figure on fixing those hands so they won't be free, eh? Well, all I've got to say is that I hope you won't spend the money foolishly, sheriff.'

Rathburn leaped lightly out of the cellar.

'Keep that other man down there covered, too,' snapped out Neal. 'It's principle more than reward money that invites me, Coyote. Hand over your gun belt an' be careful how you unbuckle it.'

'Sheriff, it would be against my code of ethics to hand over my gun. It can't be done, sheriff; you'll have to come and get it.'

Neal hesitated, notwithstanding the fact that he had Rathburn covered and that several other guns were covering him. Then he stepped forward, never taking his eyes from Rathburn's, and secured the other's weapon.

'That's better, sheriff,' said Rathburn with a queer smile. 'You can see how I have my pride an' little superstitions. No man has ever took a gun from me but what I've got it back! Thanks, sheriff.'

Lamy had come out of the cellar. Several of the men seemed to recognize him, but kept their silence with dubious looks in their eyes.

'My guide, sheriff,' said Rathburn, pointing gayly at Lamy. 'He was very kind. He showed me around the country—me not being very well acquainted around here. I had to take his gun away from him an' sort of encourage him along with my own, but he did very nicely.'

'Just what I thought, Neal,' said Brown. 'This fellow took after him an' he captured him and made him lead him. Isn't that so?' he asked of Lamy.

'Just a minute, Jud,' Rathburn interrupted with a frown. 'I can't let the importance of this momentous occasion be transferred to a subordinate. You must ask your questions of me, as I am the central figure in this affair.'

The cry of a girl startled them. She came running from the kitchen where she had fled when the sheriff announced his intention to shoot through the floor.

'Ed!' she cried, running to Lamy and throwing her arms about him. 'Oh—Ed!'

'Who is he, ma'am?' asked the sheriff 'Your husband?'

'He's my brother Ed Lamy.'

'I can recommend him if you need a guide who knows the country, sheriff,' said Rathburn genially. 'I guess he had an idea of making trouble for me at first, but I had the drop on

77

him an' he soon saw reason. I had to knock him down last night when he got fresh, but he did very well. Of course I had an advantage on my side.' He nodded toward his gun which the official still held in his hand.

'Did he make you guide him?' Neal asked Lamy, noting his empty holster.

Rathburn turned so that he could look at his former captive.

Lamy nodded. 'Yes,' he replied. 'I didn't know what minute I was goin' to get shot in the back.'

Rathburn's eyes glowed with an amused light. 'I didn't have any idea of shootin' him, sheriff; he was too valuable as my escort on the tour. I wonder if the lady could spare me a cup of coffee an' a biscuit?'

He glimpsed the boy in the kitchen doorway behind the sheriff 'Hello, sonny,' he called cheerfully. 'Did you catch those freckles from your brother?'

The boy gazed at him abashed. There were actually tears in the youngster's eyes. Ed Lamy and his sister moved into the kitchen and took the boy with them. The girl had nodded to the sheriff.

'She'll get you something to eat,' said Neal. 'What have you got on you?' He stepped to Rathburn's side.

'Ah—the frisk. I see you are a regulation officer, sheriff.' Rathburn's tone fairly radiated politeness and good cheer. 'The silver was rather heavy. It ain't my usual style to pack much silver, sheriff. There's more of the bills in my hip pockets. Don't suppose there's more'n a thousand in the whole bundle.'

The sheriff put the bills and silver on the table. He investigated all of Rathburn's pockets, returned him his tobacco, papers, and handkerchief, but kept a box of matches. Then he felt his prisoner's clothing to make sure that he had no weapons concealed; he also felt his boot tops.

He looked at Rathburn with a gloating expression when he had finished; there was also a glint of admiration in the gaze he directed at him.

'You size right up to the descriptions of you, Coyote,' he reflected in a pleasant voice. 'Too bad you couldn't have been in a better business. I'm glad I caught you, but I ain't any too—too—well, I might say any too proud of it. That may be pleasant for you to hear. But I ain't discounting your well-known ability, an' I want to warn you that I or any of my men will shoot you in your tracks if you start anything that looks suspiciouslike.'

Rathburn yawned. 'Sheriff, your courtesy is very greatly appreciated. I only hope we will arrive in jail or somewhere soon where I can get some sleep. I'm all in.'

CHAPTER ELEVEN

FREEDOM BEHIND BARS

In the early afternoon the little cavalcade rode into Dry Lake. Rathburn was nodding in his saddle, nearly asleep.

'We'll keep him here tonight till I can get the facts straight,' he heard Sheriff Neal say to Brown.

They dismounted at a small square stone building with bars on the windows. Then Rathburn was proudly led between a line of curious spectators into jail.

Three rooms comprised Dry Lake's jail. The front of the building, for a depth of a third of the distance from the front to the rear, was divided into two of these rooms; one, the larger, being the main office, and the other, much smaller, being the constable's private office. The balance of the building was one large room, divided into two old-fashioned cages with iron and steel bars. The doors to these cages were on either side of the door into the front office and there was an aisle between the cages and the wall separating them from the offices.

Rathburn was taken immediately to the cage on the left of the office door. Sheriff Neal hesitated as he stood in the cell with him, thought for a minute, then removed the handcuffs.

'That's right fine of you, sheriff,' said Rathburn sleepily, but cheerfully, nevertheless.

'Oh, you'll be watched well enough,' said Neal as he closed the barred door behind him and locked Rathburn in. 'You'll find somebody around if you try to tear the place down.'

'That wasn't just what I was getting at, sheriff,' said the prisoner with a glitter in his eyes. 'I meant it was right fine of you to give me freedom behind the bars.'

Rathburn's taunting laugh rang in the official's ears as the latter pushed the men with him into the outer office. Rathburn listened, yawning, to the sheriff giving instructions that the prisoner be watched constantly.

He looked about the cage which was separated from the other cell by a wall of sheet iron. It contained nothing except a bench and a stool. He pushed the bench against the stone wall at the rear and reclined upon it, using his coat for a pillow. Then he turned his face toward the wall, shading his eyes from the light, which filtered through two windows high in the wall beyond the bars on the left side by tipping his hat over his face.

Immediately he fell asleep.

*　　*　　*

The news that The Coyote had been captured

spread rapidly through the town and many came to the jail hoping they might be able to see the prisoner. All of these were denied admittance, but Sheriff Neal told the few who stated that they had been among the number the bandit had lined up at the point of his guns, that they would be called to identify The Coyote on the following day. He asked each if they were sure the bandit had two guns, and the reply in each case was in the affirmative.

'That's funny,' Neal muttered. 'He only had one gun on him.'

'More'n likely the other's on his horse with his saddle,' Brown pointed out. 'I believe he left his horse somewheres an' made that fellow Lamy take him to the house thinking he could get something to eat there, and that they wouldn't be so likely to be seen in the open on foot. You got to remember that man's more or less clever.'

This explanation satisfied Neal, and in the minds of the men who had been in the resort when it was held up, there was no question as to the identity of the robber. Even if they had suspected otherwise it is doubtful if they would have acknowledged it because they considered it less of an ignominy to be held up by the notorious Coyote than by a bandit of lesser reputation.

Thus did the bonds of evidence tighten about Rathburn while he slept through the late afternoon and the twilight.

When he awoke a faint yellow light dimly illuminated his surroundings. He lay thinking for several minutes. He knew night had fallen and surmised that he had slept a full eight hours. He could tell this because he was fully awake and alert. He turned noiselessly on his bench and saw that the light came from a lamp burning near the door to the outer office.

Rathburn could hear the hum of voices, and by listening intently, ascertained that two men were talking, one of whom was the sheriff. He could not recognize the voice of the other speaker as a voice he had ever heard before, and he could not hear what they were saying.

He listened dully to the voices until he heard a horse's hoofs in front of the jail. He turned back with his face to the wall, and his hat tipped over his eyes, as a man entered the jail office with a stamp of boots and jingle of spurs.

'Hello, constable,' he heard the sheriff say. 'What luck?'

'Couldn't find the hoss,' came a disgruntled voice. 'Looked all afternoon an' till it got dark for him.'

'Confound it!' exclaimed Neal. 'The horse must have been somewhere aroun' close. He sure didn't *walk* down the valley.'

'That's probably right,' said the other. 'I left a couple of your men out there to keep up searching when daylight comes. That feller Lamy showed us about where they left the hosses—his hoss an' The Coyote's—but they wasn't there. He said there was a bunch of wild hosses in the valley an' that they'd probably got away an' gone with 'em. We saw the wild hosses, but we couldn't get anywhere near 'em—couldn't get near enough to see if any of 'em was wearin' saddles or not. We had some chase while it lasted, I'll recite.'

'Did Lamy say how they came to leave their horses?' asked the sheriff in an annoyed tone.

'It was The Coyote's orders. Thought they'd be safer in the middle of the posse or something like that. Made Lamy leave the hosses an' run for the house an' made him get down in the cellar with him. Don't know if he knew Lamy lived there or not, but reckon it wouldn't have made any difference.'

The sheriff was pacing the floor of the office as his footfalls attested. 'I've ordered that Lamy in tomorrow. I've a lot more questions to ask him. Well, you might as well get a few winks, constable; Brown and the rest of 'em have hit the hay. Even the prisoner is tired out, and that's sayin' something for as tough a bird as *he* is. But I wish I had his horse. I've got to have his horse!'

Rathburn was smiling at the wall. He heard Neal walk to the door and look in. Receding footsteps told him that the constable was leaving. For a time there was silence in the outer office.

Rathburn sat up quietly and began easing

off his right boot. The boot came slowly, very slowly, as Rathburn worked at it, careful not to make any noise. Then, just as it came free, the sheriff again strode to the door and looked in.

He saw Rathburn yawning, as the boot dropped on the floor.

Rathburn looked at the sheriff sleepily as the official strode into the aisle and peered in between the bars. He tipped the bootless foot back on its toes as he lifted his other foot and tugged at the boot.

'That you, sheriff?' he asked with another yawn. 'The lights are so bad I can't see good. Guess I'm a little groggy anyway. I was too danged tired when I went to sleep to take off my boots.'

'You've got another ten hours to sleep,' said Neal with a scowl. 'An' you'll have plenty of time to get rid of your saddle soreness. You'll ride in automobiles and trains for a while an' keep in out of the hot sun an' the wet.'

The sheriff laughed harshly at his own words.

Rathburn let the other boot drop. 'I expect I'll get something to eat now an' then, too?'

'Feel hungry?' asked Neal.

'Might chaw on a biscuit before I take another nap,' yawned the prisoner.

'I'll see if I can scare you up a bite,' said the sheriff, leaving.

Rathburn heard him say something to some one in front. Then the sheriff went out of the building. The other man came in and looked at Rathburn curiously.

He was of medium build, with white hair and a face seamed and lined and red. Rathburn instantly recognized in his jailer a man of the desert—possibly of the border country.

'So you're The Coyote,' said the jailer in a rather high-pitched voice.

Rathburn winked at him. 'That's what they say,' he replied.

'You size up to him, all right,' observed the man of the desert. 'An' I can tell quick enough when I get a good look at you an' inspect your left forearm. I've had your descriptions in front of my eyes on paper an' from a dozen persons that knowed you for three years!'

'You been trailing me?' asked Rathburn curiously.

'I have; an' it ain't no credit to this bunch here that they got you, for I was headed in this direction myself an' arrived 'most as soon as you did.'

'You from Arizona?' asked Rathburn, grasping his right foot in his left hand.

'I'm from Arizony an' Mexico an' a few other places,' was the answer. 'I've helped catch men like you before, Coyote.'

Rathburn frowned, still keeping his hand over his right foot. 'I don't like that word, Coyote,' he said softly, holding the other's gaze between the bars. 'A coyote is a cowardly breed of animal, isn't it?'

'An' a tricky one,' said the jailer. 'I ain't sayin' you're a coward; but you're tricky, an' that's bad enough.'

'Maybe so,' agreed Rathburn. 'Ah—here's our friend, his nibs, the sheriff. He went out to rustle me some grub. He wants to keep me fat for hanging!'

His laugh rang through the jail, empty save for himself and the two officers. But the temporary jailer hesitated, looking at Rathburn's eyes, before he turned to the sheriff.

'Open the door and I'll take it in to him,' ordered the sheriff. 'Can't get this stuff through the bars. You might keep him covered.'

The jailer's hand flew to his hip for his gun as he also brought up a large key on a ring. He unlocked the door to the cage and held it open while he kept his gun trained upon Rathburn.

The sheriff entered and placed the food on the stool and a large bowl of coffee on the floor beside it. Then he backed out, watching Rathburn keenly as the latter sat on his bench with his right foot in his hand.

When the door clanged shut and the key rattled in the lock, Rathburn let down his right foot, took two steps, and pulled the stool to the bench. He stepped back and secured the coffee. Then he began to eat and drink, keeping his right foot tipped on its toes, while the two officials watched him attentively.

'Sheriff,' said Rathburn suddenly, between bites on a huge meat sandwich, 'could you let me have a stub of a lead pencil an' a sheet of paper to write a letter on?'

'Easy enough,' answered Neal. 'Course, you know all mail that goes out of the jail is read by us before it's delivered—if it's delivered at all.'

'I'll chance it,' snapped out Rathburn.

As the sheriff left to get the writing materials, with the jailer following him, doubtless for a whispered confab as to what Rathburn might be wanting to write and its possible bearing on his capture, the prisoner hastily ran his left hand down into his right sock and with some difficulty withdrew a peculiar-shaped leather case about ten inches long and nearly the width of his foot. This he put within his shirt.

When the officials returned he had finished his repast and was waiting for them near the bars with a smile of gratitude on his lips.

'This may be a confession I'm going to write,' he said, grinning at Neal. 'It's going to take me a long time, I reckon, but you said I had something like ten hours for sleep, so I guess I can spare two or three for this effort at literary composition. I figure, sheriff, that this'll be my masterpiece.'

His look puzzled the sheriff as he took the pencil and paper through the bars and returned to his bunk. He drew up the stool and sat upon it. It was a little lower than the bench, so, putting his paper on the bench, he had a fairly good makeshift desk. He began to write steadily, and after a few minutes the sheriff and jailer retired to the office.

It did not take Rathburn a quarter of an hour to write what he wished on the first of the several pieces of paper. He tore off what he had written, doubled it again and again into a small square, took out his sack of tobacco which he had been allowed to retain, and put it therein with the loose tobacco.

Then he wrote for a few minutes on the second sheet of paper.

When the sheriff looked in later he evidently was slowly and laboriously achieving a composition.

Rathburn heard the sheriff go out of the front door a few minutes later. Instantly he was alert. He drew on his boots. He surmised that the sheriff had gone out for something to eat and, though he wasn't sure of this, it was true.

'Oh, jailer!' he called amiably.

The wrinkled face of the desert jailer appeared in the office doorway.

Rathburn looked about from his seat on the stool. 'This job ain't none too easy, as it is,' he complained. 'As a writer I'm a first-rate cow hand. Lemme take your knife to sharpen this pencil with. When I asked the sheriff for a stub of a pencil he took me at my word.'

'Sure I'll let you have my knife,' said the jailer sarcastically. 'How about my gun—want that, too?'

'Oh, come on, old-timer,' pleaded Rathburn. 'The lead in this pencil's worn clean down into the wood.'

'Hand it over here an' I'll sharpen it,' said the jailer, drawing his pocketknife.

Rathburn walked to the bars and held out the pencil. An amiable smile played on his lips. 'You'll have to excuse me,' he said contritely. 'I forgot it wasn't jail etiquette to ask for a knife. But I ain't had much experience in jail. Now according to his nibs, the sheriff, I'm in to get pretty well acquainted with 'em, eh?'

He watched the jailer as he began sharpening the pencil.

'Speaking of knives, now,' he continued in a confiding tone, 'I got in a ruckus down near the border once an' some gents started after me. One of 'em got pretty close—close enough to take some skin off my shoulder with a bullet. He just sort of compelled me to shoot back.'

'I suppose you killed him,' observed the jailer, pausing in his work of sharpening the pencil.

'I ain't saying,' replied Rathburn. 'Anyways I had a hole-up down there for a few days, an' as luck would have it, I had to put up with a Mexican. All that Mex would do was argue that a knife was better than a gun. He claimed it was sure and made no noise—those were his hardest talking points, an' I'll be danged if there isn't something in it.

'But what I was gettin' at is that I didn't have nothing to do, an' that Mexican got me to practicing knife throwing. You know how slick those fellows are at throwing a blade. Well, in the couple of weeks that I hung aroun' there he coached me along till I could throw a knife as good as he could. He thought it was great sport, teaching me to throw a knife so good, that a way.

'Since I left down there I've sort of practiced that knife-throwing business now and then, just for fun. Anyways I thought it was just for fun. But now I see, jailer, that it was my luck protecting me. Anything you learn is liable to prove handy some time. *Don't move an inch or I'll let you have it!'*

Rathburn's hand snapped out of his shirt and up above his right shoulder.

The man from the desert shuddered involuntarily as he saw the yellow light from the lamp play fitfully upon a keen, white blade.

CHAPTER TWELVE

AGAINST HIS ETHICS

Rathburn's eyes held the other's as completely as would have been the case if he were invested with a power to charm in some occult way. Moreover, every trace of his amiable, confiding smile was gone. His gaze was hard and cold and gleaming. His face was drawn into grim lines. When he spoke he talked smoothly, rapidly, and with an edge to his words which convinced his listener that he was in deadly earnest.

'I'm not used to jails, my friend, an' I don't aim to stay here. You're not very far away an' these bars are wide enough for me to miss 'em; but I don't think I could miss you.'

The jailer looked in horror at the gleaming knife which Rathburn held by its hilt with the blade pointing backward. The jailer was from the border; he knew the awful possibilities of a quick motion of the wrist in that position, a half turn of the knife as it streaked toward its target. He shuddered again.

'Now just edge this way about two steps so your holster will be against the bars,' Rathburn instructed. 'I can drop you where you stand, reach through the bars an' drag you close if need be; but I'm banking on you having some good sense.'

The jailer, without moving the hands which held the pencil and his pocketknife, sidled up against the bars.

Rathburn leaned forward. Keeping his right hand high and tipped back, ready for the throw, he reached out with his left, just through the bars, and secured the jailer's gun.

'Now it's all off,' he said quietly. 'If the sheriff or anybody else comes before I get out of here I'm just naturally going to have to live up to the reputation for shooting that they've fastened on me. Unlock the door.'

The jailer wet his lips with his tongue. The pencil and pocketknife fell to the floor. Covered by his own gun, now in Rathburn's hand, he moved to the door, brought out his key, and opened it. Still keeping him covered, Rathburn backed to the bench, snatched up his coat, and walked out of the cage, motioning to the jailer to precede him into the office.

There he slipped the gun in his holster and put on his coat. The jailer reckoned better than to try to leap upon him while he was thus engaged; the prisoner's speed with a six-gun was well known.

Rathburn drew a peculiar leather case from within his shirt, put the knife in it, and stowed it away in a pocket. Then he turned on the jailer.

'Maybe you think that was a mean trick—

resorting to a knife,' he said pleasantly; 'but all is fair in love and war and when a man's in jail. You better sort of stand in one place while I look around a bit.'

He backed behind the desk in the big office, opened two or three drawers, and brought out a pair of handcuffs. He moved around in front of the jailer again.

'Hold out your hands,' he commanded. 'That's it.' He snapped the handcuffs on with one hand while he kept the other on the butt of his gun.

'You don't seem to have much to say,' he commented.

'What's the use?' said the jailer. 'I know when a man's got me dead to rights. But I'll be on your trail again, an' if I ever get within shootin' distance of you an' see you first, you'll never get another chance to pull a knife.'

'Well said,' Rathburn admitted. 'Now we understand each other. But I don't intend for you to ever get within shooting distance of me.'

Rathburn glanced casually about. 'Now it seems to me,' he resumed, 'that most of these fellows who gum up their jail breaks make a mistake by hurrying. Suppose you just walk naturallike through that door and into the cage I just had the foresight to leave. That's it—right on in.'

He turned the key which the jailer had left in the lock. 'Now you're all right unless you start hollering,' said Rathburn.

He stood quietly in the doorway between the office and the cages. The man from the desert studied him. He saw a variety of expressions flit over Rathburn's face—anger, determination, scorn, resolve. He was deliberately ignoring his opportunity to make his escape while conditions were propitious; he was waiting!

Although the jailer felt the urge to cry out in an endeavor to make himself heard outside the jail and thus bring help, something in the bearing of the man standing in the doorway made him keenly curious to watch the drama which he knew must be enacted sooner or later before his eyes, for The Coyote was certainly waiting for the sheriff.

Rathburn now drew the jailer's gun from his own holster and toyed with it to get its 'feel' and balance. He dropped it back into the holster and in a wink of an eyelid it was back in his hand. The man from the desert gasped at the lightning rapidity of the draw. Time and again the gun virtually leaped from the holster into The Coyote's hand at his hip, ready to spit forth leaden death. The jailer drew a long breath. The man was accustoming himself to the weapon which had come into his possession, making sure of it. Now he again stood moionless in the doorway, waiting—waiting—

Boots stamped upon the steps outside, and

Rathburn drew back from the doorway in the aisle before the cages.

The front door opened and a man entered.

Both the man in the cage and the man in the aisle recognized the sheriff's step as Neal closed the door, paused for a look about the office, and then walked toward the door leading into the jail proper.

The jailer opened his mouth to sound a warning, but something in Rathburn's gaze and posture held him silent. Rathburn's body was tense; his gaze was glued to the doorway; his right hand with its slim, brown, tapered fingers, hung above the gun at his side.

The sheriff loomed in the doorway. Without a flicker of surprise in his eyes he took in the situation. His lids half closed as his lips tightened to a thin, white line. He met Rathburn's gaze and knew that he now faced The Coyote in the role which had won him his sinister reputation.

'Did I mention to you that I wasn't used to jails, sheriff?' said Rathburn evenly, his words carrying crisp and clear. 'I don't fancy 'em. But I needed the sleep and the meal. Now I'm going. Do you recollect I said no one ever took my gun from me but what I got it back? I had to borrow this one from the gent in the cage. I'll take my gun, sheriff—*now!*'

Neal had watched him closely. He saw that while he was speaking The Coyote did not for an instant relax his vigilance. The merest resemblance of a move would precipitate gun play.

He turned abruptly, and with Rathburn following him closely, went into the private room off the jail office. He pointed to the other's gun which lay upon the flat desk where many had curiously inspected it.

Rathburn took it in his left hand and ascertained at a glance that it wasn't loaded. Therefore he elected to carry it in his left hand.

'I won't take a chance on feeding it right now, sheriff,' he said. 'Under the circumstances it would be right awkward. If you make up your mind to draw I'll have to depend on a strange gun.'

Sheriff Neal's eyes glittered; his lips parted just a little.

'Now if you'll walk back toward the cage, sheriff,' Rathburn prompted. 'Correct—don't stumble.'

Neal backed slowly out of the door, through the second door into the aisle before the cages, watching Rathburn like a cat.

Rathburn slipped his own weapon into his left hip pocket and with his left hand dug into his trousers pocket for the key to the cage. He didn't take his eyes from Neal's as he brought it out and inserted it in the lock. His right hand continued to hang above the gun he had taken from the jailer.

'Sheriff,' he said with a cold ring in his

voice, 'this may seem like an insult, but I'm goin' to ask you to unlock that cage and go in. You can take your time if you want, but I warn you fair that if any one should start coming up the steps outside I'll try to smoke you up.'

For answer Neal, with the glitter still in his eyes, stepped to the cage door, unlocked it, and swung it open.

He took a step, whirled like a flash—and the deafening report of guns crashed and reverberated within the jail's walls.

Neal staggered back within the cage, his gun clattering to the floor, his right hand dropping to his side.

'If I hadn't been up against a strange gun I wouldn't have hit your finger, sheriff,' said Rathburn mockingly. 'I was shootin' at your gun.'

He shut the cage door quickly, locked it, and stuck the key in his pocket. Then he threw the jailer's gun in through the bars and thrust his own weapon in its holster.

'I want you gentlemen inside, an' armed,' he said laughingly. 'If the jailer will be so good as to read what's written on the paper on the bench, he'll learn something to his advantage. Sheriff, you an' Brown were wrong in this, but the devil of it is you'll never know why.'

He left Neal pondering this cryptic sally, ran to the front door, opened it, and disappeared.

Neal clutched his injured fingers and swore freely, although there was amazement in his eyes. He could have been killed like a rat in a trap if The Coyote had felt the whim.

The man from the desert stepped to the bench and read on the sheet of paper:

If anybody ever gets to read this they will know that what I said about learning to throw a knife is true. I can do it. I've carried that knife in a special case that would fit in my sock and boot for just such an emergency as came up tonight. But I never would have throwed it. It would be against my ethics.

The man from the desert swore softly. Then he hurriedly picked up his gun and fired five shots to attract attention.

CHAPTER THIRTEEN

A MAN AND HIS HORSE

When Rathburn closed the outer door after him he plunged down the steps and into the shadows by the wall of the jail. Few lights showed in the town, for it was past midnight. He could see yellow beams streaming from the windows of the resort up the street, however, as he hesitated.

He was mightily handicapped because he

had no horse. A horse—his own horse, he felt—was necessary for his escape, but his horse was a long distance away.

Rathburn stole across the street to the side on which the big resort was situated, and slipped behind a building just as the muffled reports came from within the jail. After a short interval, five more shots were heard, and Rathburn grinned as he realized that the jailer had fired the remaining bullets in his own and the sheriff's guns.

He heard men running down the street. So he hurried up street behind the buildings until he reached the rear of the large resort, which was the place Lamy had held up.

Peering through one of the rear windows he saw the room was deserted except for the man behind the bar. Even at that distance he could hear horses and men down the street. Doubtless they were crowding into the jail where the sheriff would insist upon being liberated at once so he could lead the chase and, as Rathburn had the key, this would result in a delay until another key could be found, or Brown, who probably had one, could be routed out.

Rathburn thought of this as he looked through the window at the lonely bartender who evidently could not decide whether to close up and see what it all was about or not. But the thing which impressed Rathburn most was the presence of a pile of sandwiches and several cans of corned beef and sardines—emergency quick lunches for patrons—on the back bar. Also, he saw several gunny sacks on a box in the rear of the place almost under the window through which he was looking.

Rathburn stepped to the door in sudden decision, threw it open, and walked in. His gun flashed into his hand. 'Quiet!' was all he said to the stupefied bartender.

He scooped up one of the sacks, darted behind the bar, brushed the sandwiches and most of the cans of corned beef and sardines into it, and then slung it over his left shoulder with his left hand.

'The sheriff will return the money that was taken from here,' he said coolly as he walked briskly to the front door. 'Play the game safe; stay where you are!' he cautioned as he vanished through the door.

There were no horses at the hitching rail, but he saw several down the street in front of the jail. Men were running back and forth across the street—after Brown, he surmised.

Again he stole around to the rear of the resort; then he struck straight up into the timbered slope above the town, climbing rapidly afoot with the distant peaks and ridges as his guide.

Some two hours after dawn he sat on the crest of a high ridge watching a rider come up the winding trail from eastward. He had seen other riders going in both directions from his

101

concealment behind a screen of cedar bushes. He had watched them with no interest other than that exhibited by a whimsical smile. But he did not smile as he watched this rider. His eyes became keenly alert; his face was grim. His mind was made up.

When the rider was nearing his ambush, Rathburn quickly scanned the empty stretch of trail to westward, then leaped down and confronted the horseman.

Ed Lamy drew rein with an exclamation of surprise.

'There's not much time, an' I don't hanker to be seen—afoot,' said Rathburn quickly. 'Where's my horse?'

'He's in a pocket on a shale slope this side of the timber on a line from the house where you left him,' replied Lamy readily. 'Or you can have mine.'

'Don't want him,' said Rathburn curtly. 'You going in to see the sheriff?'

Lamy nodded. 'His orders. Say, Coyote—'

'He'll probably meet you on the way,' Rathburn interrupted with a sneer. 'You can be figurin' out what to say to him. My saddle with the horse?'

'It's hanging from a tree where you go into the pocket. Big limestone cliffs there below the shale. Say, Coyote, my sister an' kid brother was tellin' me about your visit that morning, an' I guess I understand—'

'We can't stand here talkin',' Rathburn

broke in, pulling the tobacco sack from his shirt pocket. He extracted a folded piece of paper. 'Here's a note I wrote you in jail before I left. Read it on the way in when there's no one watching you. Maybe you'll learn something from it; maybe you won't. I expect you wanted money to fix that ranch up; but you'll get further by doing a little irrigating from up that stream than by trying to be a bandit. You just naturally ain't cut out for the part!'

With these words he handed Lamy the note and bounded back up the slope. The screen of cedar bushes closed behind him as Lamy pushed on, looking back, wondering and confused, with heightened color in his face.

*   *   *

It was late that night when Lamy returned to the little ranch house. Frankie had gone to bed, but his sister was waiting up for him with a meal and hot tea ready.

He talked to his sister in a low voice while he ate. When he had finished he read the note for the third time; read it aloud, so his sister could hear.

'LAMY: I meant to take you back and give you up, for I was pretty sore. Then I saw your resemblance to your small brother by the freckles and eyes and I

103

remembered he had said something about you saying some decent things about me. I guess you thought they were nice things, anyway.

'Then I thought maybe you got your ideas about easy money from the stuff you'd heard about me, and I sort of felt kind of responsible. I thought I'd teach you a lesson by flirting with that posse and telling you that killing story to show you what a man is up against in this game. I guess I can't get away from it because they won't let me. But you don't have to start. I was going to give you a good talking to before I let you go, but I hadn't counted on the little kid in the house. I'm glad he told the truth. He'll remember that. I gave you back your gun because you hit the nail on the head when you said if I was square I'd give it to you and let you make a run for it.

'I took the money off you so if they got us I could take the blame and let you off. I can take the blame without hurting my reputation, so don't worry. I'm not doing this so much for your sake as for your kid brother and your sister. I figure you'd sort of caught on when I heard they hadn't located my horse. That was a good turn. Do me another by getting some sense. There's plenty of us fellows that's quite capable to furnish the bad examples.

'RATHBURN.'

The girl was crying softly with an arm about her brother's neck when he finished reading.

'What—what are you going to do, Eddie?' she sobbed.

'I'm goin' to irrigate!' said Ed Lamy with a new note in his voice. 'I'm goin' to build a sure-enough ranch for us with this piece of paper for a corner stone!'

*   *   *

Dawn was breaking over the mountains, strewing the gleaming peaks with warm rosettes of color. A clear sky, as deep and blue as any sea, arched its canopy above. Virgin stands of pine and fir marched up the steep slopes to fling their banners of green against the snow. Silver ribbons of streams laughed in the welcome sunlight.

In a rock-walled gulch, far above the head of Sunrise Cañon, a fire was burning, its thin smoke streamer riding on a vagrant breeze. Near by lay a dun-colored horse on its side, tied fast. A man was squatting by the blaze.

'I hate to have to do this, old hoss,' the man crooned; 'but we've got to change the pattern of that CC2 brand if we want to stick together, an' I reckon we want to stick.'

He thrust the running iron deeper into the

105

glowing coals.

CHAPTER FOURTEEN

THE WITNESS

The morning was hardly two hours old, and the crisp air was stinging sweet with the tang of pine and fir, as Rathburn rode jauntily down the trail on the eastern slope of the divide and drew rein on the crest of a high ridge. As he looked below he whistled softly.

'Juniper, hoss, there's folks down there plying a nefarious trade, a plumb dangerous trade,' he mused, digging for the tobacco and brown papers in the pocket of his shirt. 'I reckon they're carrying on in direct defiance of the law, hoss.'

The dun-colored mustang tossed his head impatiently, but his master ignored the animal's fretful desire to be off and dallied with tobacco and paper, fashioning a cigarette, lighting it, breathing thin smoke as his gray eyes squinted appraisingly at the scene below.

Winding down into the foothills, in striking contrast to the dim trails higher up, was a well-used road. It evidently led from the saffron-tinted dump and gray buildings of a mine which showed on the side of a big, bald mountain to southward. At a point almost directly below the ridge where the man and horse stood, it crossed a small hogback and descended a steep slope between lines of jack pines, disappearing in the timber farther down.

The gaze of the man on the ridge was concentrated on the bit of road which showed on the hogback and the slope beyond. A truck was laboriously climbing the ascent. But the watcher evidently was not so much concerned with the approach of the truck as with certain movements which were in progress on the hogback at the head of the grade.

Three persons had dismounted from their horses behind the screen of timber. One, a tall man, had donned a long, black slicker and was tying a handkerchief about his face.

'Juniper, hoss,' said Rathburn, 'what does that gent want that slicker on for? It ain't going to rain. An' how does he reckon to see onless maybe he's got holes cut in that there hanky?'

A second man had made his way down the slope a short distance. He took advantage of the timber which screened him from sight of the driver of the oncoming truck.

'I 'spect that's in case the truck driver should suddenly take it into his head to slide down backwards,' said the observer, speaking his thoughts aloud in a musical, bass voice. 'One in front, one behind; now how about the kid?'

As if in answer to his question the third

member of the party, evidently a boy, led the horses a short way up the hogback where a good view could be obtained of the road in both directions.

The watcher grunted in approval. 'One in front to do the stick-up, one behind to stop a retreat and get whatever it is they're after, and one on the look-out to see there ain't any unexpected guests. Couldn't have planned the lay any better ourselves, hoss.'

He was too far distant to interfere, even if he had had any desire to do so, which was doubtful from his interested and tolerant manner. Anyway it could have done no good to shout a warning, for the driver of the truck could not have heard anything above the roar of his machine, and the trio had gone about the preparations with dispatch. Already the truck was climbing the last steep pitch to the top of the hogback.

The tall man in the black slicker and mask now quickly stepped forth from the edge of the timber. The watcher above saw his right hand and arm whip out level with his shoulders. There was a glint of morning sunlight and dull metal. The truck came to a jarring stop as the driver jammed on the brakes. Then the driver's hands went into the air.

Stepping from the timber at the roadside behind the truck, the second man leaped upon the machine. The watcher grunted again as he saw that this man was also masked. The driver was disarmed and searched, then forced to clamber down from the truck into the road, where the man in the slicker kept him covered while the other quickly searched about the seat and cab of the truck. Then the second man released the brakes and dropped nimbly from the machine which plunged backward down the steep slope, crashed into the tree growth on one side of the road, and overturned.

The boy mounted and led the other two horses down the hogback in the scanty timber to the head of the grade. There the man in the slicker and his companion joined him, mounted, and the trio rode quickly along the hogback in a southerly direction and disappeared on a blind rail into the forest.

Rathburn rolled himself another cigarette with a grin as he watched the truck driver stand for some moments uncertainly in the road and then start rapidly down the slope toward his disabled machine.

'C'mon, hoss,' said the erstwhile spectator, turning his dun-colored mount again into the trail. 'So far's I can make out, this is the only way down out of these tall mountains to the east, so we might as well get going. We ain't got no business south or west. We'll be just in time to get blamed for what's happened down there.'

Whatever there might be in the prospect, the rider did not permit it to have any influence on his cheerful mood. He drew in long breaths of the stimulating air and sniffed joyously at the fragrance of the murmuring forests which clothed the higher hills. Far below the timber would dwindle, the ridges would flatten into round knolls and lose their verdure; then would come the dust and lava slopes, and beyond—the desert.

A wistful light came into the horseman's eyes. 'Home, Juniper, hoss,' he said softly. 'We've just got to have cactus an' water holes an' danged blistering heat in ours; and I don't care so much as the faded label off an empty tomato can if it's in California, or Arizona, or Nevada, so long as it's desert!'

The trail he was following wound tortuously around ridges, through the timber, into ravines and cañons; now treading close upon the bank of a swift-running mountain stream in a narrow valley, and again seeking the higher places where there were rocks and fallen trees and other obstructions. An observer would have gleaned at once that the rider was not familiar with the trail or territory he traversed.

So it was past noon when he finally reached the hogback where the outstanding event of the morning had taken place. The rider looked back up toward the divide and grinned as he rested his horse just above the scene of the holdup.

'Don't reckon they'd have heard me if I'd hollered, or seen me if I'd waved,' he mused. 'They picked out a good spot for the dirty work,' he concluded, looking about.

Shortly afterward, as he was staring down at the tracks in the road, he smothered an exclamation. Then he dismounted, picked up two small objects from the dust at the point where the trio had started on their getaway, examined them with a puzzled expression, and thrust them into a pocket.

'Queer,' he ruminated; 'mighty queer. If those silly things had been laying there in the road before the rumpus they'd have been tracked into the dust. But they was on *top* of a perfectly good hoss track. An' it don't look like there's been anybody along here since.'

He continued down the road, descending the steep slope, and came to the overturned truck. At a glance he saw it had been used for hauling supplies, doubtless to the mine he had glimpsed on the slope of the high mountain to southward. Several kegs of nails, some hardware, and some sacks of cement were scattered in the road. He remembered that the man who had climbed on the truck had only searched the driver and the cab. Anything he might have taken must have been in a small package or it would have been discernible even at that long distance.

'That outfit wasn't after no mine supplies,' Rathburn reflected as he finished his brief inspection and again mounted. 'An' they wasn't taking any chances on smoking anybody up or being followed too quick. Pretty work all

111

around. An' here's the committee, hoss!'

A touring car came careening around a turn in the road and raced toward him. He turned his horse to the side of the road and spoke to him as the animal, plainly unfamiliar with motor cars, snorted and shied.

The car drew to a stop with a screeching of brakes. The horseman raised his hands as he saw two rifles leveled at him from the rear seat. There were five men in the car besides the driver. One of the men, who had been sitting in the front with the driver, leaped from the machine and strode toward the rider.

'Calm that horse down an' climb out of that saddle,' he commanded. 'If you make any motions toward that gun you're packing, it'll make things simpler, in a way.'

The rider slipped from the saddle with a broad grin. 'Right up to form,' he sang cheerfully, although he kept his hands elevated while the other took his gun. 'My hoss'll be calm enough now that that danged thing is shut off. You must be a sheriff to be flirting with the speed limit that way an' forgetting you've got a horn.'

'Where are you from an' where was you going?' demanded the other.

'I'm from up in the mountains, but I'd never got where I was going if I hadn't seen you first the way you busted around that curve,' was the cool reply.

'Stranger,' was the next comment in a tone

of satisfaction. 'Look here, friend, I'm Mannix, deputy from High Point. You'll sail smoother if you answer my questions straight.'

The deputy motioned to two men in the car. 'Search him,' he ordered. Then he stood back, six-shooter in hand.

The stranger built a cigarette while the men were going through him. He lighted the weed and smiled quizzically while they examined the meager contents of the slicker pack on the rear of his saddle.

'See you're packing a black slicker,' said Mannix, pointing to the rough raincoat in which the pack was wrapped.

'That's in case of rain,' was the ready answer.

'What's your name?' asked the deputy with a frown.

'Rathburn.'

'Where was you heading?'

'I was aiming in a general eastern direction,' Rathburn replied in a drawl. 'Is there any law against ridin' hosses in this here part of the country?'

'Not at all,' replied the deputy heartily. 'An' there's no law against drivin' automobiles or trucks. But there's a law against stoppin' 'em with a gun.'

'So,' said Rathburn. 'You stopped because you saw my gun? An' I'm to blame for it? If I'd known you were touchy about guns down here I'd have worn mine in my shirt.'

One of the other men from the car had joined the deputy. He was looking at Rathburn keenly. Mannix turned to him.

'Look like him?' he asked.

The man nodded. 'About the same size and height.'

'This man was drivin' a truck up here that was stopped this morning,' said the deputy sternly to Rathburn. 'He says you size up to one of the men that turned the trick—one of them that wore a black slicker like yours.'

Rathburn nodded pleasantly. 'Exactly,' he said with a smile. 'I happen to be in the country an' I've got a black slicker. There you are; everything all proved up. An' yet there was somebody once told me it took brains to be a sheriff!'

There was a glint in Rathburn's eyes as he uttered the last sentence.

Instead of flying into a rage, Mannix laughed.

'Don't kid yourself,' he said grimly. 'You're not the man who held up this truck driver.'

He gave Rathburn back his gun, to the latter's surprise. Then he waved toward Rathburn's horse.

'Go ahead,' he said, smiling. 'General eastern direction, wasn't it? This road will take you clean to the desert, if you want to go that far. So long.'

He led the others back to the car which started off with a roar. It passed the truck and continued on up the road.

Rathburn sat his horse and watched the automobile out of sight. His expression was one of deep perplexity.

'By all the rules of the game that fellow should have held me as a suspect,' he soliloquized. 'Now he don't know me from a hoss thief—or does he?'

He frowned and rode thoughtfully down the road in the direction from which the automobile had come.

CHAPTER FIFTEEN

THE WELCOME

The afternoon wore on as Rathburn followed the road at an easy jog. He quickened his pace somewhat when he passed through aisles in thick timber, and, despite his careless attitude in the saddle, he kept a sharp lookout at all times. For Rathburn was carrying some gold and bills in a belt under his shirt—which had been examined and returned to him at the order of the deputy—and he had no intention of being waylaid. Moreover, the man's natural bearing was one of constant alertness. He rode for more than two hours without seeing any one.

'Strange,' he observed aloud. 'This road is

used a lot, too. Maybe the morning's ceremonies has scared all the travelers into the brush.'

But, as he turned the next bend in the road, he saw a small cabin in a little clearing to the right.

Spurred by a desire to obtain some much-needed information, he turned from the road into the clearing and rode up to the cabin. He doffed his broad-brimmed hat in haste as he saw a girl.

'Ma'am, I'm a stranger in these woods an' I'm looking for an honest man or woman to guide me on my way,' he said with a flashing smile.

Instead of returning his smile with a gracious word of greeting, the girl regarded him gravely out of glowing, dark eyes.

'Pretty!' he thought to himself. 'Limping lizards, but she's pretty!'

'Where are you from?' the girl asked soberly.

'From yonder mountains, an' then some,' he answered with a sweeping gesture.

'You rode down this morning?'

'I rode down this morning. Down from the toppermost top of the divide with the wind singing in my whiskers an' the birds warbling in my ears.' He laughed gayly, for he appreciated her puzzled look. 'I was wondering two things,' he continued solemnly.

'What might they be?' she asked doubtfully.

'First: Why isn't there more travel on this good road?' he said. 'I haven't seen a soul except yourself and a—a party in an automobile. Now on a road like this—'

'Where did you meet the automobile?' she asked in a voice which he interpreted as eager.

'Two hours an' some minutes back—and up. Near a truck which had had some trouble in the road. Perhaps you heard about it? Turned over on its side in collapse after some free-thinking gents turned their smoke wagons toward it.'

It was plain she was interested.

'Did—is the automobile still there?' she inquired with a breathless catch in her voice.

'Oh, no. After some of the passengers had had a little disrespectful conversation with me, it went on up the road. Are they scarce around here, ma'am—automobiles?'

'Not exactly,' she replied with a frown. 'They truck ore and men and supplies to and from the mine every day. The reason you've seen so few people today is because it's Sunday.'

'Thank you,' he said gallantly. 'That answers my first question. You remember, I was wondering *two* things?'

Her lips trembled with a smile, but her eyes flashed with suspicion.

'You will observe, ma'am, that I am not followed by any pack horses or heavily-laden burros,' he went on gravely, although his eyes

117

sparkled with good humor. 'Nor is there anything much to speak of in this slicker pack on my saddle. I need some new smoking tobacco, some new shaving soap, some new hair cut, a bath, a dinner, and a bed—after I've put up my hoss.'

This time the girl laughed, and Rathburn was rewarded by the flashing gleam of two rows of pearls and eyes merry with mirth. But her reciprocating mood of cheerfulness was quickly spent.

'You are only a mile and a half from High Point,' she said hurriedly. 'You can get what you want there.'

She retreated into the doorway, and Rathburn saw that the chance interview was at an end.

'*Gracias*, as they say in the desert country,' he said, saluting as he turned away. 'It means thanks, ma'am.'

He looked back as he touched the mustang with his steel and saw her looking after him with a strange look in her eyes.

'That gal looks half like she was scared, hoss,' he reflected. 'I wonder, now, if she got me wrong. Dang it! Maybe she thought I was trying to flirt with her. Well, maybe I was.'

He thrust a hand in a pocket and fingered the two objects he had picked up in the road at the scene of the holdup. Then he pulled his hat a bit forward over his eyes and increased his pace. The town, as he had half expected, came suddenly into sight around a sharp bend in the road.

High Point consisted of some two-score structures, and only a cursory glance was needed to ascertain that it was the source of supplies and rendezvous for entertainment of the several mines and all the miners and prospectors in the neighboring hills. Several fairly good roads and many trails led into it, and from it there was a main road of travel to the railroad on the edge of the desert in the east.

Before he entered the dusty, single street, lined with small buildings flaunting false fronts, Rathburn recognized the signs of a foothill town where the hand of authority rested but lightly.

He rode directly to the first hotel, the only two-story structure in town, and around to the rear where he put up his horse and left his saddle, chaps and slicker pack in the care of the barn man.

He received instructions as to the location of the best barber shop and speedily wended his way there. He found Sunday was not observed in the barber shop, nor in the resort which adjoined it.

'Any chance to get a bath here?' he asked one of the two barbers with a twinkle in his gray eyes.

He expected a snort of astonishment and a sarcastic reply.

'Sure. Want it first or after?'

Rathburn eyed the barber suspiciously. Was the man poking fun at him? Well, he was not a stranger to repartee.

'First or after what?' he asked, scowling.

'Your shave and hair cut.'

Rathburn laughed. 'I'll take it first—if you have it. An' if you have, I'll say this is a first-class barber shop.'

The barber led the way to a room in the rear of the place with a pleased grin.

An hour or so later Rathburn, with the lower part of his face a shade paler than the upper half, his dark hair showing neatly under his broad-brimmed hat, his black riding boots glistening, and a satisfied smile on his face, sauntered out of the barber shop into the resort next door.

A man was lighting the hanging lamps, and Rathburn looked about through a haze of tobacco smoke at a cluster of crowded gaming tables, a short bar, cigar counter, and at the motley throng which jammed the small room.

He grinned as he read the sign over the cash register:

FREE DRINKS TOMORROW

'Swiped in broad daylight from the grand old State of Texas,' he murmured aloud to himself.

Then he noticed a small restaurant in the

rear of the place, separated from the main room by a partition, the upper part of which was glass.

He made his way back, passed through the door, and took a seat at the counter which afforded him a view of the resort through the glass. He ordered a substantial meal and, while waiting for it to be served, studied with calculating eyes the scene in the next room.

The men were mostly of the hills—miners constituting the majority. Of professional gamblers there were many, and there was also a plentiful sprinkling of that despicable species known as 'boosters' whose business it is to sit in at the games in the interest of 'the house;' to fleece the victims who occupy the few remaining seats.

But now he saw a man who apparently was not a miner, or a prospector, nor yet a member of the professional gambling tribe. This was a tall man, very dark, sinewy. He wore a gun.

At first Rathburn thought he might be a cow-puncher, for he wore riding boots, and had something of the air and bearing of a cowman; but he finally decided that this classification was inaccurate. An officer at one of the mines, perhaps; a forest ranger—no, he didn't wear the regalia of a ranger—Rathburn gave it up as his dinner was put before him on the counter.

He fell to his meal eagerly, for he had had nothing to eat since early morning when he had broken camp high in the mountains to westward. Steak and French 'fries' began quickly to disappear, along with many slices of bread and two cups of steaming coffee. Then Rathburn looked up, and to his surprise saw that the tall, dark man was standing near the glass, studying him intently out of scowling, black eyes.

Rathburn looked at him coolly and steadily for a few moments and resumed his meal. But the other was inquisitive and Rathburn sensed, without again looking up, that he was being watched. Was this man, then, an aide of Mannix, the deputy? He doubted it.

He finished his meal, paid his score with an added cheery word for the counter jumper, rose, entered the main room of the resort, and walked directly up to the dark man who still was observing him.

'Was you thinking I was an old acquaintance of yours?' he asked pleasantly.

The other's eyes narrowed, and Rathburn thought he detected a glow of recognition and satisfaction.

'Did you have your bath?' sneeringly inquired the man.

Rathburn's brows lifted. Then he smiled queerly. 'I sure did. Why? Did I maybe keep you waiting? Was you next?'

The other's eyes blazed with wrath. 'Let me give you a tip, my friend; you ain't right well acquainted in this here locality, are you?'

Rathburn now noted that they had attracted immediate attention. The tall, dark man, then, was a personage of importance. He noted another thing, too—rather, he realized it by instinct as well as by certain mannerisms. The man before him knew how to use the weapon which hung low on his right thigh.

'If you mean was I born here, or do I live here, I'd say no,' Rathburn drawled; 'but I happen to be here at this precise time so I'd say I'm right well acquainted with it.'

A hush had come over the place. Interested faces were turned in their direction, and Rathburn sensed an ominous tremor of keen expectancy. The fine wrinkles at the corners of his eyes tightened a bit.

'This is a poor time for strangers to be hanging around,' said the dark man in a loud voice. 'The Dixie Queen pay roll has been taking wings too often.'

The implication and the murmur from the spectators was not lost upon Rathburn. His lips tightened into a fine, white line.

'Whoever you are, you've got more mouth than brains!' he said crisply in a voice which carried over the room.

The effect of his words was electric. There was a sharp intaking of breath from the spectators. The dark man's face froze, and his eyes darted red. His right hand seemed to hang on the instant for the swoop to his gun. Rathburn appeared to be smiling queerly out of his eyes. Then came a sharp interruption.

'Just a minute, Carlisle!'

Rathburn recognized the voice of Mannix, and a moment later the deputy stepped between them.

'What's the idea?' he asked coolly.

'This gentleman you just called Carlisle seems to have appointed himself a reception committee to welcome me into the enterprising town of High Point,' drawled Rathburn, with a laugh.

Mannix turned on Carlisle with a scowl, and Carlisle shrugged impatiently, his eyes still glaring balefully at Rathburn.

The deputy again confronted Rathburn. 'Had your supper?' he asked.

'Best steak I've had in two months,' Rathburn replied cheerfully.

'Horse taken care of?'

'First thing.' There was a note of derision in Rathburn's tone. 'Service at the hotel barn is high grade.'

Mannix's eyes hardened before he spoke again. He hesitated, but when his words came they were clear-cut and stern.

'Then come with me an' I'll show you where to sleep.'

'You mean in jail?' queried Rathburn.

Mannix nodded coldly.

'Sheriff,' said Rathburn, in a peculiar tone, addressing the deputy but looking over his shoulder directly into Carlisle's eyes; 'if there's one thing I'm noted for, it's for being a good guesser!'

CHAPTER SIXTEEN

THE DIXIE'S BOSS

If Mannix expected any resistance from Rathburn he soon found that none was to materialize. The deputy, a short, rather stout man of perhaps thirty-nine, with bronzed features, clear, brown eyes, and a protruding jaw covered with a stubble of reddish-brown beard, was nevertheless wary of his prisoner. He had not yet obtained Rathburn's gun, and he recognized the unmistakable signs of a seasoned gunman in the lounging but graceful postures of his prisoner, in the way he moved his right hand, in the alertness of his eye. He frowned, for Rathburn was smiling. There was a quality to that smile which was not lost upon the doughty officer.

'I take it you've got sense enough to come along easylike,' he said, with just a hint of doubt in his voice.

'Yes, I've been known to show some sense, sheriff; now that's a fact.'

'I'll have to ask you for your gun,' said the deputy grimly.

'I've never been known to hand over my

125

gun, sheriff,' drawled Rathburn. 'Now that's another fact.'

Again the tension in the room was high. Others than Mannix, and probably Carlisle, had readily discerned in the gray-eyed stranger a certain menacing prowess which is much respected where weapons are the rule in unexpected emergencies. The crowd backed to the wall.

The deputy wet his lips, and his face grew a shade paler. Then suddenly he went for his gun, as Rathburn dropped, like a shot, to the floor. There came the crack of Carlisle's pistol and a laugh from Rathburn. The deputy, gun in hand, stared at Rathburn who rose quickly to his feet. Then he thought to cover him. Rathburn raised his hands while Carlisle returned his own smoking weapon to its holster. Mannix turned and glared at Carlisle in perplexity.

'I don't know what his game is, Mannix; but he could have drawn down on you in a wink and shot you in your tracks if he'd wanted to,' said Carlisle.

'So you were taking the play in your own hands,' Mannix accused.

The deputy looked at Rathburn angrily. Then he advanced and took the prisoner's six-shooter from him. He brought handcuffs out of his pockets.

Rathburn's face went white. 'If what Carlisle says is true, it doesn't look as if I was trying to get away, does it, sheriff?' he asked coldly.

Mannix was thoughtful for a moment. 'Well, come along,' he ordered, thrusting the steel bracelets back into his pocket.

'I'll go with you,' Carlisle volunteered.

'That's up to you,' snapped out the deputy. 'I ain't asking you to.'

The trio left the place as the spectators gazed after them in wonder. There was a hum of excited conversation as the deputy and his prisoner and Carlisle passed through the door.

No word was spoken on the way to the small, two-room, one-story structure which served as a detention place for persons under arrest until they could be transferred to the county jail in the town where the railroad touched. Petty offenders served their sentences there, however.

In the little front office of the jail, Rathburn looked with interest at some posters on the walls. One in particular claimed his attention, and he read it twice while the deputy was getting some keys and calling to the jailer, who evidently was on the other side of the barred door where the few cells and the 'tank' were.

This is what Rathburn read:

REWARD

Two thousand dollars will be paid for the capture of the bandits who are responsible for the robberies of Dixie

Mine messengers in the last few months.
DIXIE MILLING & MINING CO.,
George Sautee, Manager.

Rathburn now knew exactly what Carlisle had meant when he had referred to the Dixie pay roll taking wings. He had, however, suspected it. The holdup of the truck driver also was explained. Rathburn smiled. It was a peculiar ruse for the mines manager to resort to. Could not the pay roll be sent to the mines under armed guard? Rathburn's eyes were dreamy when he looked at the deputy.

'All right, in you go,' said Mannix, as the jailer unlocked the heavy, barred door from the inside.

He led Rathburn to one of the single cells, of which there were six on one side of the jail room proper.

'Maybe you'll be ready to talk in the morning,' he said, as he locked his prisoner in.

'Morning might be too late,' Rathburn observed, taking tobacco and papers from his shirt pocket.

'What do you mean by that?' Mannix asked sharply.

'I might change my mind.'

'About talking, eh? Well, we'll find a way to make you change it back again.'

'You're a grateful cuss,' said Rathburn, grinning.

Mannix scowled. It was plain he was not

sure of his man, although he was trying to convince himself that he was.

'I don't get you,' he said growlingly.

'No? Didn't you hear that fellow Carlisle say I saved your life by not drawing?'

'He'd have got you if you'd tried to draw. That's what he thought you was going to do. You saved your skin by grabbing the floor.'

Rathburn wet the paper of his cigarette and sealed the end. 'I'm wondering,' he mused, as he snapped a match into flame with a thumbnail and lit the weed.

'It's about time,' said the deputy grimly.

'I'm wondering,' said Rathburn, in a soft voice, exhaling a thin streamer of smoke, 'if he'd have got me.'

Mannix grunted, looked at him curiously, and then turned abruptly on his heel and left. Rathburn could not see the door, but he heard the big key grate in the lock, and then the jail room echoed to the clang of hard metal and the door swung shut again.

Rathburn sat down on the bunk which was to serve as his bed. He smoked his brown-paper cigarette slowly and with great relish while he stared, not through the bars to where the dim light of a lamp showed, but straight at the opposite steel wall of his cell. His eyes were thoughtful, dreamy, his brow was puckered.

'An' there's that,' he muttered as he threw away the stub of his smoke and began to roll another. 'Somebody's been playing the Dixie Queen for a meal ticket. That sign said "robberies." That means more'n one. The truck driver was the last. Two thousand reward. An' me headed for the desert where I belong. What stopped me? I reckon I know.'

He smiled grimly as he remembered the insolent challenge in Carlisle's eyes and the reference to the bath.

After a time Rathburn stretched out on the bunk, pulled his hat over his face, and dozed.

He sat up with a catlike movement as a persistent tapping on the bars of his cell reached his ears. Blinking in the half light he saw Carlisle's dark features.

'Well, now's your chance to smoke me up good an' plenty an' get away with it,' said Rathburn cheerfully. 'I'm shy my gun which the sheriff has borrowed.'

'You figure he's just borrowed it?' sneeringly inquired Carlisle.

Rathburn rose and surveyed his visitor. 'I reckon I've got to tolerate you,' he drawled. 'I can't pick my company in here.'

'I've got your number,' snarlingly replied Carlisle in a low voice.

Rathburn sauntered close to the bars, rolling a cigarette.

'If you have, Carlisle, you've got a winning number,' he said evenly.

'Whatever your play is here, I dunno,' said Carlisle; 'but you won't get away with it as easy as you did over the range in Dry Lake.'

Rathburn's eyes never flickered as he coolly lit his cigarette with a steady hand. 'You're plumb full of information, eh, Carlisle?'

'I was over there an' heard about how you stuck up that joint an' tried to blame it on some kid by the name of Lamy,' said Carlisle, watching Rathburn closely.

'You sure that was the way of it?' asked Rathburn casually.

'No,' replied the other. 'I know the kid stuck up the joint an' you took the blame to keep him under cover. I don't know your reasons, but I guess you don't want the facts known. You broke jail. They ain't forgot *that* over in Dry Lake. There's a reward out for you over there, an' I wouldn't be surprised if there was some money on your head in Arizona, Coyote!'

Rathburn's eyes were points of red between narrowed lids.

'The Coyote!' said Carlisle in a hoarse voice of triumph. 'An' the way it looks I'm the only one hereabouts that knows it.'

'I told you you was plumb full of information,' said Rathburn.

'The Coyote has a bit of a record, they tell me,' Carlisle leered. 'There's more'n one sheriff would pay a pretty price to get him safe, eh?'

'Just what's your idea in telling *me* all this, Carlisle; why don't you tell what you know to

Mannix, say?'

'Maybe I'm just teasing you along.'

'Not a chance, Carlisle. I know your breed.'

The other's face darkened, and his eyes glittered as he peered in through the bars.

'What's *your* breed?' he asked sneeringly.

'I don't have to tell you that, Carlisle. You know!' said Rathburn with a taunting laugh.

Carlisle struggled with his anger for a brief spell. Then he shrugged his shoulders.

'I ain't going to poke at you in a cage,' he said in a more civil tone; 'an' I ain't going to tell anybody what I know. Remember that.'

'I ain't the forgetting kind,' Rathburn flung after him as he walked swiftly away.

Again Rathburn sat on the edge of the bunk and smoked and thought. After a time he went to sleep. The opening of his cell door woke him. It was Mannix.

'Come to let me out, sheriff?' inquired Rathburn sleepily.

The deputy looked at him keenly, opened the cage, and motioned to him to follow. Rathburn went with him out into the little office. It was broad day. Mannix picked up a pistol from his desk and extended it to Rathburn.

'Here's your gun, Rathburn. You can go,' he said, pressing his lips close together.

'Well, now, sheriff, that's right kind of you,' Rathburn drawled, concealing his astonishment.

'Don't thank me,' snapped out Mannix. 'This gentleman asked me to set you loose.'

For the first time Rathburn looked squarely at the other man in the office—a thin man, with a cropped mustache, beady eyes, and a narrow face.

The man was regarding him intently, and there seemed to be an amused expression in his eyes. He turned away from Rathburn's gaze.

'I don't believe I've ever had the pleasure of meeting the gentleman,' said Rathburn agreeably.

'That's George Sautee, manager of the Dixie Queen,' said the deputy with a shrug.

CHAPTER SEVENTEEN

A COMMISSION

Sautee rose and extended his hand with an affable smile. 'Will you come to breakfast with me, Mr. Rathburn?'

Rathburn took the hand with a curious side glance at Mannix. 'I'm powerful hungry,' he confessed; 'an' I don't reckon I'd be showing the best of manners if I balked at havin' breakfast with the man that got me out of jail.'

'Quite right,' admitted Sautee, winking at the deputy. 'Well, perhaps I have my reasons.

All right, Rathburn, let's be going.'

They walked out of the jail, and as they progressed up the street they were the cynosure of many wondering pairs of eyes; for the report had spread that the stranger who had been jailed was the bandit who had made away with the Dixie Queen pay roll on several occasions, and that he was a gun fighter and a killer.

They entered a restaurant just below the hotel, and Sautee led the way to a booth where they were assured comparative privacy.

'Ham an' eggs,' said Rathburn shortly when the waiter entered.

Sautee smiled again. He was covertly inspecting the man across the table from him and evidently what he saw caused him to arrive at a satisfactory conclusion.

He gave his order with a nod and a mild flourish of the hand, indicating that he would take the same.

'Oh—waiter,' called Rathburn. 'Four eggs with mine.'

Sautee laughed. It was a peculiar laugh in that it seemed to convey little mirth. It was perfunctory.

He gazed at Rathburn quizzically. 'They tell me you're a gunman,' he said in a low voice.

Rathburn's brows shot up. 'They? Who's they?'

Sautee waved a hand impatiently. 'I am the manager of the Dixie Queen. I have been around a bit, and I have eyes. I can see. I know the signals. I witnessed the play in the Red Feather last night.'

'That ain't a bad name for the place,' Rathburn mused.

'Just what do you suppose was my object in getting you out of jail?' Sautee asked seriously, leaning over the table and looking at Rathburn searchingly. 'You said last night you were a good guesser.'

'But I didn't say I was good at riddles,' drawled Rathburn.

Sautee leaned back. For a moment there was a gleam of admiration in his eyes. Then they narrowed slightly.

'The Dixie Queen has been robbed four times within the last year,' he said soberly. 'That represents considerable money. Yesterday I resorted to a ruse and sent the money up with a truck driver, but whoever is doing this thing must have got wise somehow, for the truck driver was held up, as you know, and the money taken.'

'Why not put an armed guard on that truck?' asked Rathburn with a yawn.

'I had full confidence in that ruse, and I knew the man who drove the truck could be trusted. Besides, he didn't know what was inside the package.'

'How much did they get?' asked Rathburn sharply.

'Twenty-two thousand eight hundred and

seventy dollars in cash.'

Rathburn stared at the mine manager and whistled softly. 'What's the sense in sending it up there at all?' he asked suddenly. 'Why not pay off down here in town?'

Sautee sighed with an air of resignation. 'That's been argued several times,' he complained. 'The men demand their pay in cash. They want it at the mine, for more than half of them have refused to come down here for it. It is twenty-nine miles up there to the mine, and it would take all the trucks we've got and two days to bring them down here and take them back. Besides, if we got them down here it would be a week before we could get half of them back up there and at work again.'

'But why won't they take checks?' Rathburn demanded.

'It would be the same proposition,' Sautee explained. 'There is a little village up there— pool room, soft-drink parlor, lunch room, store, and all that—and the men, or a large number of them, would want their checks cashed to make purchases and for spending money, and the cash would have to be transported so the business places could cash the checks. Then, there's another reason. All the mines over on this side of the mountains, clear down into the desert, have always paid in cash. This is an old district, and the matter of getting paid in cash has become a tradition. That's what the company is up against. We can refuse to do it, but all the other mines do it, and the Dixie Queen would soon have the reputation of being the only mine in the district that didn't pay in cash. The tradition is handed down from the old days when men were paid in gold. There was a time when a miner wouldn't take paper money in this country!'

The waiter entered with the breakfast dishes and they began to eat.

'Your mine owned by a stock company?' Rathburn inquired.

'Certainly,' replied Sautee. 'All the mines here are. What mine isn't?'

Rathburn ignored the question. 'Stockholders live aroun' here?' he asked, between mouthfuls.

'Oh—no, that is, not many,' replied Sautee with a quick glance at his questioner. 'This district is pretty well worked out. Most of our stockholders live in the Middle West and the East.' He winked at Rathburn.

'Any other mines been robbed?' Rathburn persisted.

'No, that's the funny part of it. Still—no, it *isn't* funny. We're working on the largest scale, and our pay roll is, naturally, the largest. It furnishes the biggest incentive. In addition, the Dixie Queen is the farthest out from town, and there are many excellent spots for a holdup between town and the mine. Oh, don't look skeptical. I've tried trusted messengers by roundabout trails, and guards and all that. They even held up a convoy on one occasion. I've set traps. I've done everything. But now I've a new idea, and I believe it'll work.'

He finished his breakfast and stared steadily at Rathburn who didn't look up, but leisurely drank a second cup of coffee. Sautee noted the slim, tapered right hand of the man across the table from him, the clear, gray eyes, the unmistakable poise of a man who is absolutely and utterly confident and sure of himself. The mine manager's eyes glowed eagerly.

'Yes?' asked Rathburn calmly.

'I'm going to hire, or, rather, I'm going to *try* to hire a man I believe is just as tough, just as clever, just as quick with his gun as the men who've been robbing the Dixie Queen. I'm going to hire him to carry the money to the mine!'

'So *that's* why you got me out of jail,' said Rathburn, drawing the inevitable tobacco and papers from his shirt pocket.

'Yes!' whispered Sautee eagerly. 'I want you for the job!'

'You ain't forgetting that I was suspected of that last job, are you? That's why I went to jail, I reckon.'

'You didn't have to go to jail unless you wanted to. You didn't have to stop in this town and invite arrest. Mannix let you go up there yesterday because he felt sure he could get you when he wanted you again, and he figured you'd make some break that would give him a clew to your pals, if you had any. You went to jail because you knew he didn't have anything on you.'

Sautee grinned in triumph.

'How do you know I won't beat it with the money?' asked Rathburn.

'I don't,' said Sautee quickly. 'But I'm taking a chance on it that you won't. I don't care who you are, what you are now, or what you've been; I don't care if you're an outlaw! I figure, Rathburn, that if I come out square and trust you with this mission and depend upon you to carry it out, that you'll play square with me. That's what I'm banking on—your own sense of squareness. You've got it, for I can see it in your eyes.'

'Who's Carlisle?' Rathburn asked dryly.

Sautee frowned. 'He's a—well, I guess you'd call him a sort of adventurer. I knew him down in Arizona. He follows the camps when they're good, and this one happens to be good right now, for we're improving the property. That's how he happened to come up here about a year ago. Then, when the first robbery occurred, I engaged him as a sort of special agent. He didn't make any progress, so I let him go. Since then he's been out and in, gambling, prospecting, anything—he's a fast man with his gun, and he has some claims here which he is developing on a small scale and trying to sell.'

Rathburn nodded but made no comment.

'Will you take the job?' Sautee asked anxiously.

'What do you want me to do?'

'I want you to carry a sum of money to the mine. I'm not going to tell you how much, but it will be considerable. The money which was stolen yesterday was for the pay-off today. I've got to get the cash for the men up there quick. They all know about the holdup, so there's no grumbling—yet. But there will be if they don't have their money pretty quick. We want to pay off tomorrow. I could go with a guard, but to tell you the truth, Rathburn, it's got to a point where I can't trust a soul.'

'Why not Mannix?' asked Rathburn sharply. Sautee shook his head; his beady, black eyes glowed, and he stroked his chin.

'There's another sorrowful point,' he explained. 'I tell you we're up against it here, Rathburn. The Dixie Queen people and most of the other mines are fighting the present county administration as a matter of policy. They want certain changes, and—well, keep this to yourself—privileges. Mannix has been instructed by the sheriff of this county that he is not here to act as a guard for the Dixie Queen. See?'

Rathburn frowned and built another cigarette.

'If you'll carry this package of money up to the Dixie Queen for me, Rathburn, I'll pay you five hundred dollars. Then, if you want to stay and act as our messenger right along, we'll make a deal. But I'd like to have you do this this time—make this one trip, anyway, I mean. They may try to stop you. If they do I don't believe they can get away with it. I'm banking on your ability to get through, and I think the proposition will appeal to you in a sporting way if for no other reason. Will you do it?' Sautee's eyes were eager.

'Yes,' said Rathburn shortly, tossing away his cigarette.

Sautee held out his hand. 'Go to the hotel and engage a room,' he instructed. 'Be in your room at nine o'clock tonight. Do not tell any one of our deal. I'll get your room number from the register. I'll bring the package of money to you between nine o'clock and midnight. Now, Rathburn, maybe I'm mistaken in you; but I go a whole lot by what I see in a man's eyes. You may have a hard record, but I'm staking my faith in men on you!'

'I'll be there,' Rathburn promised.

He left Sautee at the entrance to the restaurant and strolled around the hotel barn to see that his horse was being taken care of properly. He found that the barn man was indeed looking after the dun in excellent shape. Rathburn spent a short time with his mount, petting him and rubbing his glossy coat with his hands. Then he took his slicker pack and started for the hotel.

As he reached the street he saw a girl on a horse talking with a man on the sidewalk. The girl was leaning over, and the man evidently was delivering a harangue. He was gesticulating wildly, and Rathburn could see that the girl was cowering. He paused on the hotel porch as the man stepped away from the horse and looked his way. He recognized Carlisle.

Then the girl rode down the street and Rathburn started with surprise as he saw she was the girl from the cabin up the road who had directed him to town the day before. He remembered the two objects he had picked up in the road after the holdup and felt in his pocket to make sure they were there. Then he entered the hotel.

'Have you a room?' he asked the clerk pleasantly.

'Yes. More rooms than anything else today since the Sunday crowd's gone.'

Rathburn wrote his name upon the register.

CHAPTER EIGHTEEN

IN THE NIGHT

Rathburn avoided the Red Feather resort during the morning. Instead of walking about the streets or sitting in the hotel lobby or his room, he cultivated the acquaintance of the barn man, and because he knew horses—all about horses—he soon had the man's attention and respect.

Although Rathburn suspected that he already had a reputation in the town, he did not know that Carlisle was steadily adding to that reputation through the medium of veiled hints dropped here and there until a majority of the population was convinced that a desperate man was in their midst, and that Mannix had permitted him to go free for certain secret reasons.

Thus a web of mystery and suspicion was cleverly woven about Rathburn's movements.

It was not until afternoon, however, that Rathburn began to realize on his intimacy with the barn man. Then they began to talk of trails, and for more than an hour the barn man, caught in the spell of Rathburn's personality, divulged the secret of the trails leading to and from the Dixie Queen.

'The best trail, an' the straightest, if you should ever want to go up there an' look at the mine like you say,' said the barn man, 'hits into the timber behind the first cabin to the left above town.'

Rathburn nodded smilingly. It was the cabin where he had first seen the girl.

'It's 'bout twenty-nine miles to the mine by the road,' the man explained; 'but that trail will take you there in less'n twenty. Well, maybe twenty or twenty-one. Or you can go up the road till you get to the big hogback—that's where they held up the truck driver yesterday—and cut straight up the hill from the south end.'

'I guess those are the best trails from what you say,' was Rathburn's yawning comment.

'Them's the best,' the other added. 'There's another trail going out below town that follows southeast along a big ridge, but that trail's as far as the road. When you goin' up?'

'I dunno,' replied Rathburn non-committally. 'Say, I guess I know where that cabin is on the left side of the road going up. I stopped at a cabin up there coming down an' asked a gal how far it was to town—'

'That's it,' said the barn man. 'That's the one. Trail starts right back of that cabin.'

Rathburn yawned again. 'Smart-lookin' gal,' he observed, digging for his tobacco and papers. 'Who is she?'

'That's Joe Carlisle's sister. Anyway, he says she is. There's been some talk. Carlisle lives there when he ain't out in the hills or on a gamblin' trip to some other town.'

'I see. Well, old-timer, I ain't hung on the feed bag since morning, an' I'm going on a still hunt for some grub.'

Rathburn went to the Red Feather for his dinner. He was thoughtful through the meal and kept an eye out for Carlisle, but didn't see him. During the remainder of the afternoon he hung about the Red Feather and other resorts, but did not see Carlisle.

That evening, as he was returning to the hotel, he met Mannix. The deputy looked at him with a scowl in which there was a mixture of curiosity. Rathburn suddenly remembered what Sautee had said about his company being on the outs with the county administration. If such was the case, Rathburn reflected, how did it come that Sautee had been able to effect his release so easily?

He stopped as he drew alongside of the deputy.

'This man Sautee,' he drawled, looking Mannix square in the eye; 'he must have a good drag with the county seat, eh?'

The deputy's scowl deepened. 'He didn't get you out by word of mouth alone,' he said sharply. 'I haven't got anything on you, Rathburn—yet.'

Rathburn smiled. 'I reckon you're a sheriff after my own heart,' he said enigmatically, and moved on.

Mannix looked back after him for a moment, then continued on his way.

Rathburn had dinner that night at the hotel, and it was during the course of a number of pleasantries with the waitress, who thought he was looking for work, that he ascertained that Sautee had a little two-room building at the lower end of the street, the front half of which served as an office and the rear half as living quarters.

At nine o'clock he went to his room. He lighted the oil lamp, pulled down the window shade, sat down in a chair to one side of the door to wait. An hour passed with no sound save occasional footfalls in the hall and the drone of the wind in the trees outside.

Another hour had nearly been consumed in waiting when Rathburn heard some one coming up the stairs. The footfalls were soft, catlike. He could hardly hear them, and it was this fact which made him instantly alert. The footfalls now sounded in the hallway. They were nearer his room. He rose; stepped close to the side of the door. Then came a soft knock.

Rathburn suddenly opened the door, and Sautee started back, blinking his eyes. The mines manager peered about the room, then entered swiftly.

'You rather startled me,' he accused with a forced smile.

Rathburn closed the door softly and turned the key in the lock.

'I'm just taking natural precautions,' he explained.

Sautee shook his head and put a finger to his lips. 'Not so loud,' he warned. 'These walls'—he waved a hand about—'are all ears.'

He took a package from beneath his coat and handed it to Rathburn. 'Put it in your shirt,' he instructed. 'Deliver it to the office at the mine and take the book-keeper's receipt. Then report to my office here in town. I wish you luck, and I want you to know that I have the utmost confidence in you.'

'You keep such large sums on hand all the time?' Rathburn asked, putting the package in his shirt. He was mindful of the fact that a similar sum had been stolen the day before from the truck driver.

'There's a private bank here,' answered Sautee frowningly. 'He let me have it, but he's already sent to the county seat for more cash which will come by auto express tomorrow, probably. Anyway, the bank'll get most of this back, so their cash won't be short long.'

Rathburn nodded. 'Let's see,' he suggested. 'There was a little item of five hundred between us for my serving—am I right?'

'There is such an item,' snapped out Sautee; 'when you've delivered.'

'Of course,' replied Rathburn. 'I couldn't expect to be paid in advance. I'm to deliver the money at the mine and report to you for the five hundred.'

'Exactly,' said Sautee. 'Which way you figure on going up?' he asked curiously.

'Don't know much about the trails,' Rathburn answered. 'An' it mightn't attract suspicion if I just struck right out on the road.'

Sautee shrugged. 'Well, that's up to you,' he said. 'Keep your eye peeled. I don't think any one knows I drew that money from the bank, but I didn't think any one knew I stuck that package under the truck driver's seat, either.'

He turned toward the door.

'There's just one other little matter,' said Rathburn softly. 'You see nobody knows anything about this deal but you an' me. Maybe it would be best for my own protection that you scribbled something on a piece of paper to show what our arrangement is.'

Sautee scowled again, hesitated, then smiled. He drew an envelope from a pocket, extracted its contents, tore it open at each end, and wrote on the blank side:

> Due Rathburn five hundred dollars when he has delivered package intrusted to him by me at the Dixie Queen mine office.
>
> GEORGE SAUTEE.

Rathburn nodded in satisfaction as he took the slip of paper and tucked it into his shirt pocket. The wording of the note was a bit complicated, but it bore Sautee's signature. It was at least evidence that there *had* been an agreement.

'Everything set?' asked Sautee.

'All cinched up an' ready to go,' replied Rathburn.

'How soon you going to start?' asked Sautee as he unlocked the door.

'By midnight,' Rathburn answered.

Sautee held out his hand before he slipped out of the door and was gone.

Rathburn quickly busied himself with his slicker pack. He took out a gun which he changed for the gun in his holster. Then he stuck his regular gun into his waistband on the left. He took out the package and examined it. It was sealed at each end. Then Rathburn did a queer thing. He cut the string and paper near the seals and removed the small box within. He next emptied the box of its paper-wrapped contents and substituted the first thing of equal weight which he could lay his hands on—a moleskin glove which was among the things in the slicker pack. He replaced the box in its wrappings and drew from one of his pockets a small bottle of glue.

'First time I ever stole anything from a hotel desk,' he muttered to himself as he glued the paper back into place; 'but I sure had the proper hunch when I grabbed this.'

Next he retied the string, adding a piece from his slicker pack to offset the shortness where it had been cut. When he had finished the package looked exactly as it had in the first place. It would take a close inspection to learn that it had been tampered with. The original contents of the package he thrust into his hat and pulled the hat well down on his head.

Then he extinguished the light and made his way downstairs and out the lobby into the street. He went quickly around to the barn where he astonished the man in charge by saddling his horse and riding out without a word of explanation other than to toss him a five-dollar bill from the saddle.

'See you again tomorrow—maybe,' he called, grinning, as he rode into the night.

When Rathburn had passed behind the hotel and several other buildings on the same side of the street and gained the road leading westward toward the hogback, a slim shadow darted out of the trees, mounted a horse concealed some distance behind the barn, and slipped into a worn trail which nearly paralleled the road going west.

CHAPTER NINETEEN

QUICK TURNS

As he rode westward along the road at a swinging lope, Rathburn made no apparent effort to conceal his movements. The night sky was bright with stars, and, although the moon was not up, the road was clearly outlined through the marching stands of timber as he swung upward past the cabin where he had met the girl said to be Carlisle's sister.

Rathburn could not forget the look on the girl's face when she had asked him about the activities of the officer in the automobile. Nor could he forget the expression in her eyes during her altercation with Carlisle that day.

After he had passed the cabin, Rathburn checked his pace and proceeded more slowly up the long stretches of road to the hogback. On the hogback he began to take advantage of the screen of timber on the lower side of the road, and to ride more cautiously. However, to any one who might have been watching, his movements still would have been easily discernible, and it would have appeared that he wasn't quite sure of himself. Twice he turned off at what he appeared to think was the beginning of a trail, and both times he again turned back to the road.

Then, as he reached the south end of the hogback where the trail left the road and cut straight across to the mine, two horsemen broke from the timber, and Rathburn reined in his horse as the guns which covered him glinted.

The taller of the pair of night riders kept him covered with two guns while the other rode in close and jerked the weapon from his holster.

'C'mon with the package!' said this man in a hoarse voice. 'We won't take a chance on you. If you make any kind of a break you'll get it where it'll do most good.'

There was a sneering inflection in the voice.

Rathburn's hand, as it moved downward

toward his shirt, hovered an instant above where his good gun was stuck in his waistband, out of sight under the skirt of his coat; then it moved to the open shirt at his throat. He drew out the package and held it out toward the other.

The man closed in and snatched the package, glancing at it in the dim starlight.

'Now back the way you came an' don't invite no shootin'!' was the brief command.

Rathburn whirled his horse and drove in his spurs. As he fled from the scene a harsh laugh came to his ears from behind. Then utter silence save for the pounding of his horse's hoofs in the hard road back down the hogback.

'Jog along, hoss,' Rathburn crooned as he sped down the long slopes toward town; 'maybe we're peggin' things wrong, an' if it turns out that way we've a powerful long ways to go.'

It lacked a few minutes of being two hours after midnight when he reached the Carlisle cabin. There he reined in his horse, dismounted in the shadow of the timber, and crept to a window. The moon had risen and was bathing the hills in a ghostly light in which every object stood out clear-cut and easily distinguishable. Rathburn peered into the two front windows, but could see nothing. Then, from a side window into which the moonlight filtered, he made out a bedroom. It was not occupied. From the other side of the cabin he saw another bedroom, and it, too, was unoccupied.

'Nobody home,' he muttered cheerfully as he ran for his horse.

In another minute he was again speeding down the road toward town. He slacked his pace as he reached the upper end of the short main street. The street was dark save for two beams of yellow light, one of which shone from a window of the jail office and the other from the front of the Red Feather resort.

He walked his horse down the street past the jail and the resort and almost to the end of the line of buildings where he arrived before the small, one-story, two-room structure which was Sautee's office and abode.

The place was dark. Rathburn dismounted and led his horse into the dark shadow at the side of the little building. Then he went around to the front, and, drawing his gun from his waistband, he rapped smartly on the door with its butt and dropped it into his holster.

There was no movement within, and Rathburn rapped again and tried the door. It was locked.

A match flared into flame somewhere beyond the front room. A glow of light followed. Rathburn, looking through the front window, saw a door open wide and made out the form of Sautee as the mines manager came forward to the front door.

'Who is it?' Sautee called cautiously.

'Rathburn.'

After a moment a key turned in the lock and the door opened part way. Rathburn pushed his way in.

'Why—didn't you *go*?' asked Sautee in excited tones.

'Lock the door an' come in the other room,' whispered Rathburn. 'I've got something to tell you that'll knock you for a goal.'

Sautee hurriedly locked the door, and, as he turned to lead the way into the other room, Rathburn deftly extracted the key.

In the light from the lamp in the bedroom Sautee swung on his visitor and looked at him keenly. The mines manager was fully dressed, and the bed was made. It was evident that he had merely dozed on top of the covers with his clothes on. These things Rathburn noted even as Sautee surveyed him with a frown.

'Well, what is it?' snapped out Sautee.

Rathburn blinked in the light. 'I—I was held up,' he said sheepishly.

The mines manager stared. First he stared into Rathburn's eyes, and then he glanced to the gun in the holster on his thigh.

'Couldn't have been very much afraid of you,' he said sneeringly. 'I see they didn't even take your gun.'

'It all come from my not knowin' enough about the trails, I guess,' Rathburn explained lamely. 'Got me on the far end of the hogback. Two of 'em. Had their guns in my face before I

154

knew it. Couldn't have drawed if I wanted to. They'd have shot me out of the saddle in a wink. All I could do was hand over the package an' beat it.'

'And they said you were a gunman,' said Sautee in derision. 'How do I know anybody stopped you and robbed you? Maybe you've come back here with that story to cover up the theft of the money. I guess I made a mistake in ever thinking of trusting a man of your caliber.'

'I was afraid of that,' said Rathburn. 'I was afraid if anything like this was to happen you might think I was lying and was taking the money myself. But I fooled 'em, Mr. Sautee,' he finished in triumph.

'What's that?' Sautee asked sharply.

'Look here,' cried Rathburn excitedly as he took off his hat and recovered the package he had put in it before starting toward the mine.

He held up the package. 'I was scared they might get wise an' get the drop on me,' he said. 'So I opened the package an' took out what was in it and put it in my hat. They got the original package, all right, but it was stuffed with an old glove of mine. Here's the money. I didn't go right on to the mine for fear they'd find out their mistake an' pot me from the timber. This is the money you gave me, minus the seals an' the string an' box. I wanted you to see that I was on the square.'

Sautee's eyes were bulging. 'Give me that,'

he gulped out.

'Why—don't you want me to take it to the mine?' asked Rathburn in surprise.

'Hand that over,' ordered Sautee, reaching for the package.

Rathburn drew away. 'All right, Mr. Sautee,' he said in a complaining voice. 'If you don't want me to go through with the job you can back down, I guess. We'll just make sure the money's here, though.'

Sautee leaped toward him.

'Give me that package!' he cried angrily. 'Do you hear me?'

Rathburn warded him off, keeping the package at arm's length away.

'Just hold your horses,' he said coldly. 'I reckon I know what I'm doing. You don't trust me now, an' I ain't goin' to take any chances with you. I'm goin' to open this an' show you that the money's there, that's all; I'm goin' to show you that I'm giving you back what you gave me all fair an' square.'

Sautee's face was ashen. His voice trembled as he spoke again: 'Hand it over and get out of here. I've had enough trouble with you. I'll take your word for it.'

But Rathburn was undoing the paper wrappings.

Again Sautee made a leap, but this time he met Rathburn's left fist and staggered back, dropping into a chair. Rathburn looked at him coldly.

156

'Funny you're so anxious to take my word for things now, when a minute ago you said you couldn't know but what I'd told that holdup story for a blind so's I could get away with—*this*!'

The wrappings fell away, revealing a wad of blank paper.

Rathburn's face froze. Sautee stared white-faced at what the other held in his hand. Then a peculiar glint came into his eyes and he looked at Rathburn narrowly.

'So that's the way of it,' he said sarcastically.

Rathburn stuffed the paper into a pocket. Then he pulled a chair in front of the mines manager and sat down. He took out paper and tobacco from his shirt pocket and began to fashion a cigarette.

'It sure looks bad for me, doesn't it, Mr. Sautee?' he asked as he snapped a match into flame.

'I thought you were going to return the money,' Sautee said sneeringly.

'It looks bad two ways,' Rathburn went on as if he hadn't heard the other's comment. 'First, if that package the holdups got had contained the money you could have swore it was a put-up job. I'd have had to beat it fast. Now, when I find that the package you gave to me was full of blank paper, you can say that I framed the holdup story and changed the money for paper in the bargain.'

Sautee's eyes were glowing. 'An' you'll have

to beat it, after all,' he jeered.

'So it would seem,' mused Rathburn. 'I fooled 'em, an' to all appearances I fooled myself, although maybe I *did* take a peep into that package when I changed it in my room, Mr. Sautee.'

The mines manager shifted in his chair; but he stared defiantly at Rathburn.

'You'd have a hard time proving anything,' he said grimly.

'That's the trouble,' Rathburn admitted. 'I'd sort of have to depend on you. I was thinkin' maybe you double crossed me to make 'em think *I* was carrying the money while you sneaked it up some other way, Mr. Sautee.'

'You can think what you want to,' said Sautee. 'But you better start moving. If I was you, I'd get as far away from this town and Mannix as I could by daylight.'

Rathburn's manner underwent a lightning change as he threw away his partly finished cigarette.

'You're right,' he said crisply. 'It's time to start moving, Sautee.'

He rose, and his right hand moved incredibly fast. Sautee gasped as he looked into the bore of Rathburn's gun. He could hardly realize that Rathburn had drawn.

'I fooled the night riders twice,' explained Rathburn with a peculiar smile. 'First, when I let 'em get the wrong package, an' again when I let 'em get the wrong gun. This gun an' I work together like clock ticks when necessary. I'll have to ask you to fork over the money that you drew from the bank an' that should have been in that package, Sautee.'

Rathburn's eyes had narrowed and hardened; his words were cold and menacing—deadly in their absolute sincerity.

'What—what do you mean?' stammered the mines manager.

'I take it you're not deaf,' snapped out Rathburn. 'Maybe you don't know it, Sautee, but so help me, you're takin' a chance by acting like you didn't get me.'

Sautee's thin face was twitching in a spasm of commingled rage and fear.

'The Coyote!' he breathed.

'Who told you that?' demanded Rathburn on the instant.

Sautee gripped the sides of his chair, and his face went a shade more pallid.

'Carlisle,' he confessed in a strained voice.

Rathburn laughed, and the mines manager shivered as he heard.

'Now, Sautee, we'll quit beatin' around the bush,' Rathburn said through his teeth. 'We'll get down to business together, or I'll begin to search your place here. But if I have to search, I'll search alone. There ain't so much chance of a shot bein' heard way up the street; an' there ain't much chance of me bein' caught on that hoss of mine if I don't want to get caught. Also, I'm beginning to feel like I was in a hurry. Fork over that money!'

Sautee looked just an instant longer into the eyes of the man towering over him. Then he rose, shaking, dry-lipped, and knelt down by the head of the bed. He lifted a piece of the carpet, opened a small trapdoor, reached inside, and brought out a bundle of bank notes. Rathburn took the money from him.

Sautee still was kneeling as he heard Rathburn walk lightly to the front door and insert the key in the lock. He tried to cry out, but the effort resulted only in a croak in his throat. He heard the door close softly.

'The Coyote!' he mumbled, passing a hand across his forehead.

The echoes of galloping hoofs came to him as he scrambled to his feet and staggered toward the door.

CHAPTER TWENTY

APPEAL TO THE LAW

For some moments Sautee stood in the darkened doorway staring up the moonlit street. The echoes of Rathburn's flight had died away. The town was still. Sautee did not cry out, although he had recovered a considerable measure of his composure. He listened intently and finally grunted with satisfaction.

'Up the road,' he muttered. 'That means he is making for the pass over the mountains.'

He walked hurriedly through his office into the living room. There he stood for a spell beside the table on which burned the lamp. His brows were knit into a heavy frown. He seemed debating a question in his mind. He tapped with nervous fingers on the table top.

'Pshaw,' he said aloud, his face darkening. 'He's an outlaw.'

He put on his coat and dropped an automatic pistol into a side pocket. After another moment of hesitation he blew out the light and walked quickly out of the place, locking the door after him.

He hurried up the street to the jail. He found the jailer dozing in the little front office and did not attempt to disturb him. From the jail he hurried another short distance up the street and turned in at a little house located some distance back from the sidewalk. He knocked loudly on the door, and after a brief wait repeated the performance.

A light showed, and the front door opened. Mannix, the deputy, looked out.

'Let me in,' said Sautee briefly. 'There's been another robbery.'

Mannix swung the door wide and stepped aside. He wore an ulster over his night clothes, and his bare feet were thrust into slippers. He scowled at the mines manager as he shut the

161

door.

'More of the company's money gone?' he asked with a touch of sarcasm in his voice.

Sautee nodded. 'Some twenty-odd thousand,' he said soberly; 'and I believe the man that got it is responsible for the holdups that have been pulled off around here.'

'Who got it?' Mannix asked quickly.

'Rathburn,' Sautee announced.

Mannix smiled in undisgusted contempt. 'Your own fault,' he pointed out. 'Wouldn't give me a chance to investigate. Said you had a scheme that would show him up one way or the other. Wouldn't let me in on it, an' I was fool enough to let you have a try, although I don't believe I could have held him anyhow.'

'Just it,' said Sautee. 'Wouldn't have done any good to keep him in jail, and I thought I had a two-way scheme that would either show him up, as you say, or get me an excellent messenger. I intrusted Rathburn with a package to carry to the mines office. He's a gunman, a desperado, probably a killer, and I thought it would appeal to him to be put in a place of trust. If he fell down—then I figured you'd be able to get him like you said you could.'

Mannix snorted. 'After tryin' a fool scheme you want to shift the business on my shoulders, eh? Well, Sautee, you've never shown much confidence in my ability, an' you don't have to show any now. It looks to me as if the finishing of this play is all up to you.'

'Oh, no, it isn't,' said Sautee confidently. 'You'll be most mighty glad to take out after him.'

'Suppose you wait an' see how quick I start,' Mannix retorted angrily. 'What's the matter? Didn't he carry out your orders? I suppose you gave him a bundle of money to make off with. Sautee, I believe you're a fool!'

The mines manager winced and then frowned. 'I gave him the money to carry to the mine,' he confessed without flinching. 'He came back with a story about being held up, and when he saw that I didn't believe him and intended to turn him back to you, he pulled a gun on me and made his getaway. He lit out through town for the road to the hogback and the pass over the mountains.'

Mannix laughed harshly. 'You're clever, Sautee; there's no getting away from how clever you are. Now you want me to go chasing up to the hogback to head him off. Well, I'm tellin' you that I don't know where he's gone, an' I ain't starting out after him at any two o'clock in the morning. If you'd have kept your nose out of this he'd still be all safe an' quiet in jail. That's final, so you might as well clear out an' give me a chance to get some sleep.'

Sautee merely smiled after this speech from the disgusted deputy.

'Since I intrusted Rathburn with that job I've found out something about him which

163

takes the case out of my hands entirely,' he said with a smirk. 'I don't care if you don't start after him till day after tomorrow. But if your chief—the sheriff—finds out that you didn't hit the trail tonight he'll likely ask you for your badge!'

'Are you threatening me?' Mannix demanded loudly.

'No, I'm only stating facts,' Sautee replied stoutly. 'That man who calls himself Rathburn is The Coyote!'

Mannix didn't start. He appeared hardly interested. Only the keen, penetrating quality of the steady gaze he directed at the mines manager betrayed the fact that his faculties were aroused.

'The Coyote hit back for Arizona after that deal he was mixed up in over in Dry Lake, across the range,' he said with conviction.

'Oh, he did?' Sautee sneered openly. 'Well, you had him in jail last night, and you can probably get him again, if you start right out after him.'

'What makes you think this fellow Rathburn is The Coyote?' demanded Mannix.

'Carlisle knows him by sight, and he told me.'

'Then why didn't you tell me?' the deputy asked sternly.

'Because Carlisle didn't tell me until after I told him what I'd done,' Sautee evaded. 'Then I didn't have the—ah—nerve, under the circumstances, to come to you with the news. At that, I thought he might go through with it.'

Mannix swore softly. 'Giving a payroll messenger's job to a man who's got a price on his head a mile long!' he exclaimed savagely. 'Why didn't Carlisle come to me?'

Sautee shrugged. 'I'm not responsible for Carlisle. Maybe he didn't feel sure of it, and maybe he's just naturally jealous of The Coyote and wants to bring him in himself. Carlisle is a gunman, as you know, and a good one.'

'I know it,' snapped out Mannix; 'and I know both Carlisle an' you are a pair of bunglers. I guess you wanted to show me up, but you've gone about it in a way that won't get you anything nor hurt me, I'll see to that.'

Sautee smiled as the deputy hurried out of the room. In a few minutes Mannix returned fully dressed and carrying a rifle. The deputy's face was severe, and his eyes burned with the fire of the man hunt. He signaled impatiently to the mine manager to follow him. As they walked across the little porch and around to the rear of the house where Mannix kept his car the deputy talked fast.

'I'm goin' up to the hogback. He ain't had start enough to get up there yet on a horse, an' I'll beat him to it. It'll be daylight in about two hours, an' I'll be there till daylight. If you think you can do it, get out some of the men an' cover the trails to the mine on horses. He might try to get over that way. Then you better take your car and go up to the mine by the road as fast as you can to tell 'em to be on the lookout. Watch out on the hogback, for I'll be up there, parked with my lights out.'

He had reached his small garage when he finished giving his instructions, and Sautee, with a promise to do as he had been told as quickly as possible, ran down the street toward the Red Feather, where a light still shone.

The news that The Coyote and Rathburn were one and the same, and that he had robbed the mining company that night and was probably responsible for the other holdups, created an immediate sensation among the few gamblers in the resort. Sautee added to the excitement by quoting rewards at random, and the forming of two posses to comb the trails to the mine and beyond was under way at once.

Sautee ran to his office and got out his small car. He stopped at the Red Feather and took one of the men from the mine with him. He stopped again when he reached the Carlisle cabin, pounded on the doors, and looked in the windows. But the place was deserted, and Sautee's features were wreathed in perplexity as he went back to his car.

'That's queer,' he said as he climbed into his seat.

'What's that?' asked the man beside him.

But Sautee's answer was drowned in the roar of the motor as he sped up the road toward the hogback and the mine.

CHAPTER TWENTY-ONE

A CAPTURE

When Rathburn rode away from Sautee's quarters he galloped up the street straight for the road which led west out of town. He pulled his horse down to a trot when he reached the Carlisle cabin and made another brief inspection which showed that the place was deserted. Then he struck into the trail behind the cabin and began the ascent toward the Dixie Queen.

He rode slowly through the timber, depending upon his mount to keep to the dim trail, but in the open stretches in meadows and on the crest of ridges where the timber thinned, he made better time. On this occasion one would not have noted an attitude of uncertainty about his manner or movements. He had paid strict attention to the barn man's description of this trail, and he had determined general directions the day before. Rathburn was not a stranger to the art of following new trails; nor was he the kind to become confused in a locality with which he was not familiar unless he became absolutely lost. In this instance it would be a hard matter to become lost, for the ridges rose steadily upward toward the summits of the high mountains, the town was in the narrow valley below, and the foothills ranged down to the desert in the east.

He was halfway to the mine when he saw the gleam of an automobile's lights in the road far below.

'Sautee got busy right quick,' he said aloud. 'I 'spect they're hustlin' up to head me off at the hogback. They're figuring I'd try to go back the way I come in.'

He smiled grimly in the soft moonlight, and his gaze turned toward the east, where the stars glowed over the shadowy reaches of desert which he could not see, but the very thought of which stirred something in his soul.

Then he pushed on up the trail toward the mine. For more than an hour he rode, and then, when he came to the crest of a ridge just below the Dixie Queen, he saw the lights of an automobile in the road to the right of him.

'Now what?' he ejaculated. 'They ain't figurin' I'd come up here!'

He sat his horse with features again wreathed in perplexity. He scowled at the approaching gleam of light. In the direction of the hogback he could see nothing. Nor could he see the horsemen already on the trail below him and on the ridge trail to eastward.

The little mine village was directly below him. The few buildings huddled together below the big mine dump were dark. The mine buildings, too, were dark. A faint glow showed in the east—harbinger of the dawn.

The left side of the automobile was toward him when it stopped in the little street below. A man climbed out and walked around in front of the car, and Rathburn grunted in recognition as he made out the familiar form of Sautee, the mine manager.

He saw Sautee and another leave the car and walk toward a building at the lower end of the street. He could see them fairly well in the moonlight and realized that in a comparatively short time it would be daylight. He turned his horse down the slope.

When he reached the rear of the few buildings which formed the mining village, catering to the wants of the Dixie Queen workers, Rathburn edged along to the lower end where he left his horse in the shadow of a building directly across from the one which Sautee and his companion had entered, and in the windows of which a light now shone.

He stole across the street. Peering in one of the windows he saw that the room was an office. Sautee was standing before a desk, talking to another man. Rathburn quickly surmised that this man had accompanied Sautee from the town. Even as he looked, Sautee finished his speech by striking a palm with his fist, and his companion strode toward the door.

Rathburn darted around the side of the building into the shadow as the man came out and hurried up a wide road toward the mine buildings above. Then Rathburn ran around to the front of the building and quietly opened the door.

Sautee had seated himself at the desk, and he swung about in his chair as he heard the door open. He looked again into the black bore of Rathburn's gun. His eyes bulged, and this time they shone with genuine terror.

'It was sure in the pictures for us to meet again, Sautee,' said Rathburn easily. 'Our business wasn't finished. We ain't through yet.'

'There isn't any more money,' Sautee gasped out. 'There's no money up here at all.'

'Oh, yes, there is,' said Rathburn with a mirthless smile. 'There's twenty-odd thousand dollars in my right-hand coat pocket. Now I wonder what you've got in yours. It don't stand to reason you'd start out this time without a gun. Stand up!'

Sautee rose. His face was ashen. He held his hands high as Rathburn pressed his weapon against his chest and relieved him of the automatic which he carried. Rathburn felt his other pockets and then smiled agreeably. He tossed the automatic on the desk.

'All right, we'll get goin',' he announced, indicating the open door. 'We'll have to hurry, for I take it you've sent for somebody from the mine.'

'Where are we going?' asked Sautee without moving.

'We're goin' for a little mornin' walk, if you act reasonable,' replied Rathburn. 'That was my intention. But if you don't want to go—'

He shrugged, and as Sautee looked fixedly at him, he cocked his gun.

Sautee hurried toward the door with Rathburn following him closely. When they were outside Rathburn directed Sautee across the street. When they reached Rathburn's horse Rathburn quickly mounted and motioned to the mines manager to precede him into the timber behind the little village. When they gained the shelter of the timber they gradually circled around until they struck a trail which led up above the mine. They started up this, Sautee leading the way on foot with Rathburn following on his horse and keeping his gun trained on the mines manager's back.

'Don't worry,' Rathburn croned. 'I won't shoot you in the back, Sautee. That wouldn't be accordin' to my ethics. But I'd have to stop you if you made a break to leave the present company.'

Sautee plodded on, his breath coming in gasps, the perspiration standing out on his forehead.

The trail joined with another well-worn path a short distance above the mine. The eastern sky now was light, and Rathburn saw a stone building above them. He also saw that they were on the steep slope of the big mountain on which the Dixie Queen was located, and that there was a rift in this mountain to the left which indicated the presence of a pass there.

In a few minutes they reached the stone building. It had an iron door across which was painted the legend:

DANGER
POWDER—DYNAMITE
KEEP AWAY

Rathburn dismounted and tossed the reins over his horse's head so the animal would stand.

'That place looks like a natural jail,' he commented.

'It's the mine's powder house,' said Sautee, wiping his wet forehead.

'Sure,' Rathburn rejoined, 'that's just what it is. I expect there's enough powder in there to blow half this mountain off.'

He walked to the door and took out his gun as he examined the padlock.

'What are you going to do?' asked Sautee excitedly.

'I'm goin' to blow the lock off,' said Rathburn coolly.

'Don't do it!' cried Sautee. 'There's high-percentage dynamite in there and TNT caps

172

that we use on road work—dozens of boxes of it. You might set it off!'

Rathburn looked at the quaking mine manager speculatively. 'That's right,' he said finally, turning aside to grin to himself. 'I guess any little jar might start it workin'. It goes off easy, I've heard.'

'There are caps and detonators in there, too,' said Sautee quickly. 'You might shoot into them some way, you never can tell. Well, it would be as bad for you as for me.' He uttered the last sentence in a note of triumph.

Rathburn was looking at the far-flung view below. He turned a hard gaze on Sautee. 'What difference do you suppose it would make to me if that stuff in there goes off?' he demanded in a harsh voice. 'Look down there!'

Sautee looked and drew in his breath with a gasp.

In the clear light of the blossoming dawn the whole panorama of the lower mountain country was spread out before them. To the left, under the towering peaks of the divide, the rounded crest of the hogback was discernible, and a black spot marked the location of Mannix's automobile.

'There's a car over there,' said Rathburn, noting the direction of Sautee's gaze.

Almost directly below them a number of mounted men filed over a ridge and again disappeared in the timber. Off to the right more horsemen were to be seen.

'Looks like there was a posse or two out this morning,' said Rathburn in a forbidding voice. 'I reckon I ain't such a fool as not to know who they're lookin' for, Sautee. Now maybe you can figure out why I ain't as scared of that powder house as you are.'

'I can stop them!' cried Sautee in a shaking voice.

'Sure,' Rathburn agreed. 'You can say you lied about me takin' the money—'

'I'll tell 'em you gave it back!' said Sautee hoarsely. 'I'll tell 'em you brought it on up to the mine and that it's in the safe. I'll square it—'

'But you can't square the rewards that are out for The Coyote,' said Rathburn sternly. 'You've stepped into a bigger game than you thought, Sautee, an' its got plumb out of your hands.'

He turned on the mine manager fiercely. 'Whatever happens, remember this: Once a man gets a bad reputation in a country like this or the country I come from, he's got it for keeps. He can't get away from it no matter how he acts or what he does. Mine has drove me away from the place where I belong; it's followed me here; I can't lose it; an' the way things has been going, by glory, I don't know if I *want* to lose it!'

Sautee cowered back under the fierceness in Rathburn's manner.

'An' you can tell 'em, if you ever have a chance to talk again, that I earned my reputation square! I ain't involved nobody else, an' I ain't stole from any poor people, an' I never threw my gun down on a man who didn't start for his first.'

The deadly earnestness and the note of regret in Rathburn's tone caused Sautee to forget his uneasiness temporarily and stare at the man in wonder. Rathburn's eyes were narrowed, his gaze was steel blue, and his face was drawn into hard, grim lines as he looked out upon the far-flung, glorious vista below them, broken here and there by the movement of mounted men.

'Maybe I—I—' Sautee faltered in his speech. His words seemed impotent in the face of Rathburn's deadly seriousness.

Rathburn turned abruptly to the powder-house door.

'Wait!' cried Sautee.

The mines manager dug frantically into his pockets and drew out a bunch of keys.

'There are some locks on this property to which there are only two keys,' he explained nervously. 'This is one of them, and I carry the second key. Here!'

He held out the key ring with one key extended.

Rathburn thrust his gun back into its holster and took the keys. In a moment he had unlocked the padlock and swung open the iron door, exposing case after case of high explosive within the stone structure.

Sautee was staring at him in dire apprehension.

Rathburn pointed toward the rift in the mountain on the left above them. Sautee looked and saw a man and a boy riding down the trail.

'That looks to me like the man that held me up last night,' said Rathburn. 'He looks like one of the men, anyway. Maybe he's found out he didn't get much, eh? Maybe he's coming back because he didn't have enough to make a getaway with. Maybe he thinks he was double crossed or something.'

Sautee's features were working in a spasm of fear and worry. Suddenly he turned on Rathburn.

'Why don't you get away?' he asked in eager pleading. 'That trail will take you out of the mountains and down into the desert country. You're from the desert, aren't you? You can make it. You've made a good haul. Go! It'll be better for me and all of us!'

Rathburn laughed bitterly. 'I can't go because I'm a worse fool than you are,' he said acridly. 'Get in there. Sneaking lizards, man, can't you see I'm tempted to put a shot into one of them boxes and blow us both to kingdom come?'

Sautee shrank back into the powder house, and Rathburn slammed the door.

As Rathburn snapped the padlock and thrust the keys into his pocket his eyes again sought the trail to the left above him. No one was in sight. The man and the boy had disappeared in a bend or depression in the trail.

But when he looked down toward the hogback he saw a car coming up the road toward the mine. A number of horsemen had taken its place on the hogback.

Rathburn ran for his horse.

CHAPTER TWENTY-TWO

A SECOND CAPTURE

Rathburn rode straight up the trail which led from the powder house toward the pass over the big mountain. His eyes were gleaming with satisfaction, but several times they clouded with doubt, and he felt the bank notes in his coat pocket. Each time, however, he would shake his head and push on up the trail with renewed energy.

Looking backward and downward, he could see the posses gathering in the street of the mine village. He sensed the excitement which had followed the sudden disappearance of Sautee and smiled grimly. He saw that the automobile from the hogback had reached the village. Scores of men were clustered about it. He knew Mannix was taking personal charge of the man hunt; but there was a chance to get away!

He looked wistfully eastward. Somewhere off there, beyond the rolling foothills, was the desert. He thrilled. It had been there he had made his first mistake. Goaded by the loss of his small cattle ranch he had taken revenge on the man who had foreclosed on him and others in a similar predicament. He had held up the bank and restored a small measure of the losses. Even then the profit of the unscrupulous money lender had been enormous.

But the law had marked Rathburn. The gunmen who were jealous of his reputation as an expert at the draw had forced him to fall back upon that draw to protect his life. Thus he had been driven to obtain a living in the best way he could, and something in the dangerous, uncertain life of the outlaw had appealed to his wild blood.

Sautee had said the money in his pocket was a good haul. Why not? He looked again to eastward. Over the big mountain—into the timber—a circling back—a straight cut east—

He knew he could do it. He had evaded posses before—posses composed of trained men who were accustomed to take the man trail. It would actually be rare sport to play with the crowd below. His left hand dropped idly into his coat pocket, and he started as he fingered what was there. Then his brow became furrowed, and he scowled.

'Maybe I ain't such a good guesser after all,' he muttered. 'Maybe I'm just what I told Sautee—a fool.'

He caught sight of a man and a boy above him. Another instant and they were lost to view.

Rathburn suddenly put the spurs to his horse, and the dun surged up the steep trail. As he rode, Rathburn took his rawhide lariat from its place on the saddle. At a point above where the trail twisted about a huge out-cropping of rock he turned off, dismounted, and crept to the top of the rocks. Quickly he surveyed the trail above. Then he slipped back down to his horse, got in the saddle, and took up a position just at the lower end of the outcropping, some little distance back from the trail and above it. He held the lariat ready in his hands.

He sat his horse quietly—listening. The wind had died with the dawn, and there was no sound in the hills. The sun was mounting in the sky to eastward. Rathburn looked out over the timbered slopes below with wistful eyes. Suddenly his gaze became alert. The sound of horses upon the rocky trail above the outcropping came to his ears.

Gradually the sound became more and more distinct. He could hear the hoofs of the horses striking against the rock of the trail. He shook out the noose of his rope, and it sang as it whirled in the air.

The head of a horse had hardly pushed past the rock when Rathburn's noose went swirling downward and dropped true over its target. The man in the saddle loosed a string of curses as he felt the rawhide lariat tighten about his arms and chest. His horse shied, and he was dragged from the saddle, landing on his feet, but falling instantly.

The second horse reared back, and Rathburn's gun covered the boy in the saddle. Rathburn, keeping tight hold on the rope hand over hand, and retaining his gun in his right hand at the same time, ran down the short pitch. The boy's horse became still, and while the youth stared Rathburn trussed up the first rider and then stood off to look at him.

'Just takin' a mornin' ride, Carlisle?' he asked cheerfully. 'Or did you forget something? Don't make any false moves, kid. I ain't in a playful mood.'

The boy continued to stare, but Carlisle's face was black with rage, and curses flowed from his lips.

'That won't get you anything,' Rathburn said coolly. 'You might better be doin' some tall thinking instead of cussing. You ain't got the cards stacked for this deal, Carlisle.'

'What's your game?' Carlisle managed to get out.

'It's a deep one,' Rathburn replied dryly. 'An' it's too complicated to tell you now. I'm goin' to give you a chance to do the thinking I mentioned a while back. I ain't takin' your gun or your horse. The only thing I'm takin' is a chance, an' I ain't takin' it on *your* account.'

For an instant Rathburn's eyes burned with fury. Then he dragged Carlisle into the shelter of the rocks, to the side of the trail, and tied his horse near by. Mounting, he motioned to the boy to ride down the rail ahead of him. He looked at the big hat and the overalls the boy wore. The youth looked wildly about and then drove the spurs into his mount and dashed down the trail with Rathburn close behind, calling to him to take it easy.

Just as they reached a spot directly above the powder house the boy reined in his horse. Rathburn saw he was looking down at the turbulent scene in the street of the little village below the mine. Then the boy swayed in the saddle, and Rathburn had just time to fling himself to the ground and catch the senseless form in his arms as it toppled.

He put his burden down on the grass beside the trail and led his horse into the timber and tied him. Next he picked up the boy and made his way down to the powder house. The shouts of many men came to him from far below. He succeeded in getting out the keys and unlocking the padlock which secured the door of the powder house. Then he opened the

181

door, covered the frightened mine manager with his gun, and carried his burden in with one arm.

'One of the accomplices,' he said briefly to Sautee, as he put the lad down and loosened the shirt at the throat. 'He'll come around in a minute.'

Sautee's eyes were popping from his head. He leaned back upon the cases of dynamite and passed a clammy hand over his brow.

'I've got Carlisle, too,' said Rathburn. 'Takin' it all around from under it ain't a bad morning's haul.'

Sautee now stared at him with a new look in his eyes—a look in which doubt struggled with terror.

'I don't believe you *are* The Coyote!' he blurted out.

'Who do you reckon I might be, if I ain't?' Rathburn asked quietly.

'You might be some kind of a deputy or some thing.'

Rathburn laughed harshly. 'It just happens I'm the man some folks call The Coyote,' he said. 'I don't like the name, but it was wished on me, an' I can't seem to shake it off. If I wasn't the man you think I am you wouldn't be in such a tight fix, Sautee.'

Rathburn's words conveyed a subtle menace which was not lost on the mine manager. Sautee cringed and rubbed his hands in his nervous tension.

'What are you going to do?' he asked.

'Listen!' exclaimed Rathburn.

From below came the echoes of shouts and other sounds which conveyed the intelligence that a large body of men was on the move up to the mine and the mountain slope above.

'They're after me,' said Rathburn bitterly. 'They think I stole the pay rolls. They can't get me, Sautee—not alive. An' if they get me the other way I'm goin' to see to it somehow that I don't get blamed for these jobs up here. Now, do you begin to see daylight?'

Sautee wet his dry lips. The figure on the floor stirred. The shouts from below sounded more distinct.

Rathburn's gun leaped into his hand. 'You better start hoping the shootin' don't begin till we understand each other, Sautee,' he said grimly. 'We've come to the show-down!'

CHAPTER TWENTY-THREE

QUICK FACTS

Disregarding the sounds which continued to come from below, Rathburn stood, gun in hand, regarding Sautee with a grim countenance and a cold look in his keen, gray eyes.

'I saw that truck driver held up, Sautee. I

183

was on a ridge below the divide. I saw the tall man in the black slicker, his pardner, an' the boy. I didn't figure it would do any good to tell Mannix I'd taken in the show, an' I was on my way to the desert. I'd be there now if Carlisle hadn't overstepped the mark in that Red Feather place.'

Sautee pricked up his ears. 'You let them arrest you,' he said. 'Why—'

'Because I knew Mannix didn't know who I was an' didn't have anything on me,' said Rathburn quickly. 'An' I got peevish at Carlisle an' plumb suspicious when he tried to make things look bad for me right there at the start. I began to wise up to the whole lay when you got me out of jail.'

Sautee's face went white again.

'Your fine explanations of why you couldn't get that money up to the mine were thin as water, Sautee. You could get that money up there if you wanted to, an' when you asked me to carry the package to the mine it was a dead out-an'-out give-away. I reckon you didn't play me to have any sense, an' I don't think you gave Carlisle credit for havin' the brains of a jack rabbit, either.'

Rathburn laughed as the mine manager stared at mention of Carlisle's name again.

'Don't worry,' he said contemptuously. 'I know it was Carlisle who held me up. I take it he figured that you'd actually put money in that package. Wouldn't be surprised if it was

184

him that you got to try that stunt. An' he started away with the package as soon as he got it instead of sneakin' back home to split with you. He double crossed you an' you double crossed him an' me. Now I'm double crossing the two of you.'

Sautee's look had changed to one of anger. He glared at Rathburn, forgetting his predicament.

'You'd have a fine time proving any of this nonsense,' he found the courage to say.

'I'm not only goin' to prove what I've said so far, but I'm goin' to prove that these robberies were a put-up job between you an' Carlisle, with somebody helping you,' said Rathburn. 'I've been in the mining game myself, Sautee, but in our country men spend their lives hunting metal to make some bunch of stockholders rich. Maybe they get something out of it themselves, an' maybe they don't; but they're square, an' the men that run the mines are square 'most always. Anyway they develop properties, an' that's more'n you're doing. You're not doing this camp any good. You're bleeding the mine an' the company, too.'

'And I suppose you—The Coyote—are taking a hand in this business as a matter of principle,' sneeringly replied Sautee.

'I didn't take a hand,' Rathburn pointed out sternly. 'You an' Carlisle forced a hand on me, an' I'm goin' to play it out. I've another reason, too,' he added mysteriously.

185

'Did you say you had Carlisle?' Sautee asked in feigned anxiety.

'I've got him dead to rights,' replied Rathburn shortly, taking some paper and a pencil from a pocket.

Sautee looked at him curiously as he started to write on the paper. 'Going to write it all out and leave it?' he asked sneeringly.

'I'm going to put it outside the powder house in a place where Mannix or some of the others will be sure to find it,' was the puzzling answer.

'I suppose they'll believe it quicker if it's in writing,' said Sautee bravely.

Rathburn finished writing, folded the paper, and placed it in the left-hand pocket of his coat. He carefully put away the pencil. His next act caused Sautee real concern.

Using a drill which was there for the purpose, evidently, Rathburn broke open a box of dynamite caps and a box of dynamite. A single coil of fuse was lying on a box. He quickly affixed the cap to a stick of the dynamite and crimped on a two-foot length of fuse. Then he moved the opened box of dynamite to the doorway and struck the stick with cap and fuse attached into it.

'There,' he said, evidently greatly satisfied with his work. 'That fuse will burn about two minutes—' He paused. 'That's too long,' he concluded.

Perspiration again stood out on Sautee's

forehead as he watched Rathburn cut off a foot of the fuse.

'That's better,' said Rathburn with a queer smile. 'That'll burn about a minute. Time enough.'

Sautee stared in horrified fascination at the foot of fuse which stuck straight out from the box of dynamite in the doorway. 'What—what are you going to do?' he gasped out.

'Listen, Sautee,' said Rathburn coolly. 'When that stick of powder explodes it'll set off the box an' the other boxes, an' instead of a powder house here there'll be a big hole in the side of the mountain.'

'Man—man—you're not going to do—*that*!' Sautee's words came in a hoarse whisper.

'I reckon that's what I'm goin' to have to do,' said Rathburn as he bent over the form on the floor of the powder house.

The boy's eyes were open and were staring into Rathburn's.

Rathburn lifted him to his feet, where he stood unsteadily. Again the gun was in Rathburn's hand.

'This party is goin' to leave us,' he said to the frightened mine manager. 'I'm goin' to step just outside for a minute. It's your chance to make a break, Sautee; but if you try it I'll send a bullet into that cap. Maybe you heard somewhere that I can shoot tolerably well,' he concluded in his drawl.

Sautee gripped the sides of the boxes piled

187

behind him.

Rathburn led the boy outside and said quickly: 'Just what is this man Carlisle to you?'

A look of fear, remorse, dejection—all commingled and pleading—came into the dark eyes that looked up into his.

Rathburn didn't wait for a verbal answer.

'Your horse is just up the trail a piece,' he said hurriedly. 'Get up there—go up behind the powder house, so the men below can't see you. Swing off into the timber to the left and get down out of here. I'll keep their attention. Go home.'

He waited a moment until he saw that his instructions were being carried out, then he leaped again to the doorway of the powder house.

Sautee's face was livid, and his teeth were chattering. Rathburn took a match from his shirt pocket.

'Stop!' screamed Sautee. 'I'll talk. You were right. It was a frame-up. I'll tell everything— *everything*!'

The perspiration was streaming from his face, and his voice shook with terror.

'You'll have a chance to talk in less than a minute,' said Rathburn calmly.

A chorus of shouts came from the trail just below the powder house as a number of men came into view.

Rathburn stepped in front of the door with the match in his left hand and his gun in his right.

CHAPTER TWENTY-FOUR

THE SHOW-DOWN

A wild chorus of yells greeted him. He had surmised that the men had seen him coming back down the trail to the powder house with his human burden. Now he called Sautee into view. They would most naturally assume that it was the mine manager he had been carrying.

'Come to the door where they can see you,' he called to Sautee.

The ring in his voice brought Sautee, white-faced and shivering, to the doorway beside Rathburn.

Another round of yells followed the mine manager's appearance. Then there was a sudden stillness. Rathburn saw that the crowd was made up mostly of miners. They paused in the wide place in the trail just below the powder house, and Mannix pushed to the fore.

'I want you, Coyote,' he called sternly.

'Now, don't you think I know it?' replied Rathburn in a voice which carried to all the members of the mob. 'You don't want me for robbing this mine, Mannix; you want me for something you don't know anything about— because I've got a record. Wait a minute!'

He shot out the words as the mob pushed a step forward.

'If you fellows take a couple more steps in this direction I'll put a bullet into this box of dynamite!'

The movement stopped instantly. Men stared up at him breathlessly, for they realized that he meant what he said.

Mannix's face was pale, but his eyes glowed with determination.

'Do you think it's worth it, Coyote?' he asked.

'Step up here, Mannix, an' listen to what this fellow has to say,' was Rathburn's reply. 'Men,' he called in a loud voice, 'I'm lookin' to you to give your mine boss an' your deputy sheriff a fair deal.'

There was a murmur among the men. Mannix, after a moment of hesitation, stepped forward.

Rathburn swung on Sautee. 'Tell him!' he commanded in a voice which stung like the crack of a whip on still air.

'I—I had a hand in the business,' said Sautee frantically. 'It was Carlisle and me. We—we framed the robberies.'

Mannix's eyes narrowed.

'Tell him where I got that money last night,' Rathburn thundered. 'Tell him, Sautee, or, so help me, I'll drill a hole through you!'

Sautee cowered before the deadly ferocity in Rathburn's voice. 'I had it in the—office—downtown,' he stammered. 'There was blank paper in that package, Mannix. Let him go—

let him go, Mannix, or we'll all be killed!' Sautee cried.

Rathburn was looking steadily at the deputy. 'Carlisle is roped an' tied up the trail by the big rocks,' he said. 'Send up there for him an' bring him down here.'

Several of the men who were mounted spurred their horses up the steep trail. There was utter silence now among the men. Mannix, too, was cool and collected. He had not drawn his gun. He surveyed the quaking Sautee with a look of extreme contempt. The mine manager's nerves had gone to pieces before Rathburn's menacing personality. All he cared for now was his life. The black reputation he had given to Rathburn led him to believe that the man could not be depended upon, and that he was liable to carry out his threat and blow them all to bits. He wet his lips with a feverish tongue.

'Where's the money you an' Carlisle got away with?' demanded Mannix.

'I've got all I took,' whined Sautee. 'I'll give it back. I don't know what Carlisle's done with his. It was his scheme, anyway; he proposed it when he hit this country a year ago.'

'And the other man—' suggested Mannix.

'Mike Reynolds,' cried Sautee. 'But he was only in on the truck driver deal and—last night. Let The Coyote go, Mannix—'

Then Sautee, in a frenzy of fear, an easy prey to the seriousness of the situation and his shattered nerves, told everything. He explained how it had been Carlisle who proposed getting Rathburn out of jail and making him the goat. He told of the worthless contents of the package he had given Rathburn to carry to the mine, how they had planned to rob him on the way and thus put him in a situation where he would have to get out of the country. He explained how Carlisle had pointed out that they had a club over Rathburn's head in their knowledge of his real identity. He complained that Carlisle had intended to double cross him, and how he had double crossed Carlisle in turn. He ended with a whining plea for consideration at the hands of Mannix.

The men with Carlisle came down the trail. Carlisle was astride his own horse. His gun was in his holster.

'We've got you, you outlaw!' he cried as he flung himself from the saddle and strode up to Rathburn, Mannix, and Sautee.

Rathburn's eyes had narrowed until they were slits through which his cold, hard gaze centered upon Carlisle. His attitude had changed. Even his posture was suddenly different. There was a long breath from the men behind Mannix. It was a tense moment. They could see the menace in Rathburn's manner, and they could see that Carlisle was fighting mad.

'Ain't you a little free with your language,

Carlisle?' drawled Rathburn.

'You know who he is?' Carlisle cried to Mannix. 'He's The Coyote—an outlaw an' a killer with a price a mile long on his head—'

'But I ain't never sneaked any miners' pay rolls, Carlisle,' Rathburn broke in with a sneering inflection in his voice. 'What'd you do with Mike Reynolds? He was with you last night, wasn't he?'

Carlisle's jaw snapped shut. He swung on Rathburn with eyes darting red. Then his gaze flashed to the cringing Sautee.

'You—you rat—'

Rathburn stepped before Sautee. 'You haven't any quarrel with him, Carlisle,' he said evenly; 'your quarrel, if you've got one, is with me. I outguessed you, that's all. You ain't plumb clever, Carlisle. You ought to be in a more genteel business. I just naturally figured out the play an' made Sautee talk, that's all. I ain't the only gent Mannix is wanting—there's *three* of us here!'

Carlisle's face was purple and working in spasms of rage. He realized instantly that Rathburn had spoken the truth.

'It was his scheme from the start!' shrilled Sautee from the protection of Rathburn's broad shoulders.

Then the mine manager, unable to longer stand the strain, collapsed on the ground, groaning.

'Underhanded!' Carlisle shot through his

teeth as Mannix stepped back. 'An' I heard The Coyote was a go-getter. By guns, I believe you're yellow!'

'You've got a chance to try an' finish what you started in the Red Feather the day I got here, Carlisle,' said Rathburn in ringing tones. 'If you think I'm yellow—draw!'

A second's hesitation—two figures in identical postures under the morning sun—a vagrant breeze murmuring in the timber.

Then two movements, quick as lightning—too fast for the eye to follow—and the roar of guns.

Rathburn stepped back, his weapon smoking at his hip, as Carlisle swayed for a moment and then crumpled upon the ground. Rathburn quickly drew the piece of paper from his left pocket and the roll of bills from his right. He put the note with the bills and tossed the roll to Mannix. Then he stepped back to the doorway.

'Join your men, Mannix,' he said quietly.

Mannix thrust the money into a pocket and stood for several seconds looking directly into Rathburn's eyes. A curious expression was on the deputy's face, partly wonder, partly admiration, partly doubt. Then he turned abruptly upon his heel and walked back to the gaping men.

Sautee struggled to his feet. Rathburn motioned to him to join the others, and he staggered down to them.

Then Rathburn coolly lit a match and touched it to the fuse sticking out from the box of dynamite.

There was a wild yell of terror, and the mob tumbled down the trail as Rathburn ran for the trail above the powder house. The men had disappeared when he turned. His gun leaped into his hand and he fired—once, twice, three times—the fourth shot cut the burning fuse, and with a sharp intaking of breath, he ran for his horse, mounted, and rode into the timber along the trail.

CHAPTER TWENTY-FIVE

FILED!

Rathburn picked his way slowly through the timber around to the southeast and then directly down toward the town. It was slow going, and the man seemed to relish this fact. His face was thoughtful, wistful, a bit grave. He occasionally patted his horse's neck.

'We're on our way home, old hoss,' he said softly. 'Seems like we just *had* to stop off here.'

He fingered two small objects in his coat pocket.

'I wonder,' he murmured. 'I wonder if I could be mistaken.'

He turned west after a time and rode

carefully until he gained a worn trail. This he followed down toward town, and in half an hour he dismounted in the timber behind a small cabin at the side of the road to the hogback.

Rathburn went to the rear door and knocked. He received no answer, but sounds came to him through an open window. He opened the door softly and stole inside. There was no one in the kitchen. The sounds came from another room. He passed on into a bedroom and turned into another bedroom where he saw a figure in overalls lying on the bed. A great mass of dark hair covered the pillow. The form shook with sobs.

Rathburn laid a gentle hand upon the shoulder, and the face, which was quickly turned to him, was the face of a girl—the girl he had first seen when coming into the town, the girl who had been sitting the horse listening to Carlisle's tirade, the girl the barn man had said was supposed to be Carlisle's sister.

'They don't know you were up there,' said Rathburn softly. 'Your boy's clothes fooled them, if they saw you at all. They probably thought I was carrying Sautee down the trail, for they found Sautee up there in the powder house with me.'

The girl sobbed again. Her eyes were red with weeping.

'Listen, ma'am,' said Rathburn gently. 'I

picked these up from the road the day the truck driver was held up.' He brought out two hairpins from his coat pocket.

'It set me to thinking, ma'am, an' was one reason why I stayed over here to find out what was goin' on. Maybe I've done wrong, ma'am, but I was hoping I'd be doin' you a favor. I saw the look in your eyes the day Carlisle was talkin' to you when you was on the hoss. I know you helped him in his holdups, dressed like a boy, but I figured you didn't do it because you wanted to.'

'No—no—no!' sobbed the girl.

'All right; fine, little girl. No one knows anything about it but me, an' I'm goin' away. But, listen, girlie, just what was Carlisle to you?'

A spasm of weeping shook the girl. 'Nothing I could help,' she sobbed. 'He—I had to do as he said—because—oh, I hate him. I hate him!'

'There, there,' soothed Rathburn. 'I suspected as much, girlie.'

'He made my father a bad man,' sobbed the girl; 'an' made me go with him or my father would have to go—to—to go—'

'Never mind, girlie,' Rathburn interrupted softly. 'I don't want to hear the story. Just keep it to yourself an' start all over. It ain't a bad world, girlie, an' there's more good men in it than there's bad. Now, you can begin to live and be happy like you ought. Carlisle won't worry you no more.'

She raised her head and looked at him out of startled eyes in which there was a ray of hope. 'You say—he won't—worry me—'

'Not at all, girlie. He walked into his own trap. I'm goin', girlie. So long, an' good luck.'

He took her hand and pressed it, and under the spell of his smile the hope came into her welling eyes.

'Good-bye,' he called from the doorway.

She was smiling faintly through her tears when he slipped out.

*   *   *

Deputy Sheriff Mannix was sitting in his little office alone. It was nearly sunset. A faint glow of crimson shot across the carpet.

Mannix was scowling thoughtfully. On the desk before him were two pieces of paper. One of them was a reward notice publishing the fact that The Coyote was wanted and that five thousand dollars would be paid by the State of Arizona for his capture, dead or alive.

Mannix picked up the second piece of paper and again read the words penciled upon it:

I am taking out of this money belonging to the Dixie Queen the five hundred dollars Sautee promised me for carrying the money to the mine, and the two thousand dollars reward offered for the capture of those who had been

198

robbing the Dixie Queen. I expect that shortly after this gets into the proper hands Sautee will be in jail, and he will be handy to tell you this is all O.K.

RATHBURN.

Mannix took up the reward notice, put it with the note, and jammed the two pieces of paper into an obscure pigeonhole in his desk.

'Filed!' he said aloud.

Then he rose with a peculiar smile, went out upon the little porch, and stared toward the east where the reflection of the sunset cast a rosy glow over the foothills leading down to the desert.

CHAPTER TWENTY-SIX

THE PRODIGAL

With face upraised to the breath of air which stirred across the bare black lava hills, Rathbun leaned forward in the saddle eagerly, while his dun-colored horse stood patiently, seemingly in accord with his master's mood. A merciless sun beat down from a hot, cloudless sky.

Below, stretching in endless miles was the desert—a sinister, forbidding land of desolate distances, marked only by slender yucca palms, mesquite, dusty greasewood, an occasional clump of green palo verde, the slim fingers of the ocatilla, the high 'forks' of the giant sahuara, and clumps of la cholla cactus, looking like apple orchards in full bloom.

Yet the man's gaze fell for a moment lovingly on each species of cactus and desert vegetation; his look was that which dwells in the homesick eyes of a traveler when he sees his native land from the deck of an inbound ship.

'Hoss, we're home!' he said aloud, while the animal pricked up its ears.

Then he looked off to the left, where the blue outlines of a low range of mountains wavered in the heat like a mirage.

'Imagination Range,' he said moodily.

He tickled the dun with his spurs and trotted along the crest of the lava ridge. At its eastern terminus he swung down into the desert and struck straight east in the direction of Imagination Range. The desert's surface between the lava ridge and the higher hills of the range to eastward was cut by dry washes and arroyos and miniature ridges studded with giant cactus.

On the top of one of these high rises the horseman suddenly reined in his mount and stared into the south. 'There's trouble—an' spelled with a capital T!' he ejaculated.

The gaze in his keen gray eyes centered upon a number of riders speeding their horses over the tumbled section of desert below him to his right. He made out two divisions of horsemen. One group was some distance ahead of the other. Even as he stared down at them, its group separated, and some rode for Imagination Range, while others hastened toward the lava hills, or due north in his direction. The second group halted for a brief spell, evidently for a conference, and then its members also divided and started in swift pursuit of the men ahead.

The watcher on the top of the rise frowned.

'Out of here, hoss,' he said sharply. 'This ain't our day for visitors.'

He pushed on eastward, increasing his pace, but losing time in skirting the frequent bits of high ground. As he rode down into a deep arroyo, a horseman came galloping into its lower end and raced almost upon him before seeing him. His hand darted like lightning to his gun, and the weapon snapped into aim at his hip. The horseman came to a rearing halt, reins dangling, his hands held high, his eyes bulging from their sockets.

'Rathburn!' he exclaimed.

'The same,' said the man with the gun. 'What's all the disturbance down there?'

'Bob Long is chasing us,' the other answered with a nervous grin.

'As I remember it,' drawled Rathburn, 'Bob Long is the sheriff of Mesquite County. You boys sure ain't been misbehaving?'

'It's worse than that,' said the fugitive, staring doubtfully at his questioner. 'The stage driver's dead. Had a notion the boss was foolin' when he told him to reach up for the bugs in the air.'

'Who does the boss happen to be in this case?'

The man hesitated.

'Take your time,' said Rathburn sarcastically; 'there's nobody after you but the sheriff, an' he probably won't be along for a minute or two.'

'It won't do *you* no good for him to find us here,' said the other boldly.

Rathburn's eyes blazed. 'I reckon you're forgettin' that Bob Long knows I travel alone,' he said hotly. 'He savvys I don't travel with a crowd. I ain't found it necessary so far, an' I ain't aiming to start. I counted eight in your gang—to hold up one stage, eh?' He concluded with a sneer, while the other shifted nervously in his saddle and cast a quick look back over his shoulder. There seemed no one there.

'You needn't be lookin' around,' Rathburn said coldly. 'You're goin' to stay here till you answer my question, if all the sheriffs in Arizona come ridin' up meanwhile. Who's headin' your gang?'

'That ain't professional,' the fugitive grumbled. 'You're just the same as one of us.'

Then, seeing the look that came into

Rathburn's eyes, he said hastily: 'Mike Eagen planned the lay.'

'I guessed it,' said Rathburn in a tone of contempt. 'Well, you better slope while you've still got a chance.'

He motioned to the man to go, and the latter rode at a gallop up the arroyo and out of sight. Rathburn's face wore a worried scowl, as he slid his gun into its holster, whirled his horse, and speedily climbed the east side of the arroyo.

From a vantage point he caught sight again of the horsemen racing up from the south. They were much nearer, and he could readily make out the members of the sheriff's posse. He had had experience with posses before.

Striking around the crest of the high ground which formed the east side of the arroyo, he again raced toward the range of mountains in the east, taking advantage of every bit of cover which offered concealment from the riders approaching at top speed from the south.

Occasional glances made it plain that the sheriff was sending, or personally bringing, most of his posse east in the direction of the mountains, presumably in the hope of cutting off the outlaws from seeking refuge in the hills. But the mountains were Rathburn's goal as well as the goal of a majority of Mike Eagen's band, though for totally different reasons. He refused to change his direction, although by going north, the stout, speedy dun could doubtless outdistance the posse before the afternoon was spent.

Rathburn's teeth snapped shut, his jaw squared, and his eyes narrowed, as he saw indubitable signs that he had been detected. Two of the posse were waving their arms and dashing in his direction. At that distance they could not identify him, but under the circumstances such identification was unnecessary. His presence there, riding like mad, was certain to convince the pursuers that he was one of the gang responsible for the stage job. This was obvious.

For good reasons, Rathburn did not want it generally known that he was back in a country where he had spent most of his life, and where he was branded as a desperate outlaw with a big price on his head. Consequently, seeing that the sheriff's men were out to get him, he abandoned all attempt at concealment, drove in his spurs, gave the dun horse its head, and raced for the mountains.

Other members of the posse who were farther to the east caught the signals of the two who were in pursuit of Rathburn, and they dashed north to cut him off. The outlaws had disappeared, and Rathburn shook his head savagely, as he realized they had sought cover when they saw the chase was directed at one man. Without having had a hand in the holdup of the stage, he had arrived on the spot just in time to draw the fire of the authorities. And fire it was now; for the men behind him had begun shooting in the hope of a chance hit at the distance.

A scant mile separated him from his goal. He came to a level stretch which was almost a mass of green because of the clumps of palo verde. Here he urged the dun to its utmost, outdistanced the pair in his rear, and gained on the men riding from the south, almost ahead of him. He swerved a bit to the north and cut straight for a notch in the mountains. He smiled, as he approached it, and saw a narrow defile leading into the hills. He gained it in a final, heartbreaking burst of speed on the part of his mount. As he dashed into the cañon, bullets sang past him and over his head. Then a cry of amazement came to his ears.

'It's The Coyote!' a man was yelling. 'Rathburn's back!'

He dashed into the shelter of the defile, a grim smile playing on his lips. He had been recognized. His face hardened. He rounded a huge boulder, checked his horse, and dismounted. He could hear the pound of hoofs in the entrance of the narrow cañon. A rider came into view below.

Rathburn leaned out from the protection of the boulder. His lips were pressed into a fine, white line, and there was a look of haunted worry in his eyes. His gun flashed in his hand. The rider saw him and yelled, spurring his horse. Then Rathburn's gun swung quickly upward. A sharp report sounded, like a crash of thunder in the narrow confines of the cañon, and its echoes reverberated through the hills.

The rider toppled in his saddle and fell to the floor of the cañon. His horse came to a snorting stop, reins dangling, all four legs braced. The hoofbeats instantly were stilled. A silence, complete and sinister, reigned in the defile.

Rathburn slipped his smoking gun into his holster and mounted noiselessly. Then he walked his horse slowly up the cañon, sitting sidewise in the saddle to keep a vigil on the trail behind. A minute later he heard a volley of shots below, the signal to all the scattered members of the posse to race to the entrance of the cañon. He increased his pace, broke his gun, extracted the empty shell, and inserted a fresh cartridge in its place.

CHAPTER TWENTY-SEVEN

THE DESERT CODE

Keeping to the trail, Rathburn mounted higher and higher and spoke continually to his horse in a crooning tone of encouragement. His face was drawn in grim lines, his eyes were constantly alert, his very posture in the saddle showed that his nerves were at high tension.

He ignored dim paths which occasionally led off to the left or right in rifts in the sheer, black walls of the narrow cañon. No sound came to him from below. He knew the posse would have to proceed with the utmost caution, for the sheriff and his men could not be sure that they would not encounter him at some bend in the trail. They would be expecting shots from every boulder; for Rathburn had let them know he had no intention of being taken easily or alive.

The afternoon wore on, with Rathburn steadily penetrating the very heart of Imagination Range. Finally he swung out of the cañon trail and took a dim path to the right. He dismounted and walked back to rub off the scars left by his horse's shoes on the rock floor of the side trail. Satisfied that he would leave the members of the posse confused as to which side trail he had taken, he returned to his horse, mounted, and proceeded up the narrow trail leading to the top of the range to the south of the deep cañon.

In the western sky the sun was low when he rode down the crest of the range. The mountains were devoid of vegetation, bleak and bare and black. The lava rock seemed to absorb the heat of the sun and throw it in the rider's face. But Rathburn didn't appear to mind it.

He crossed the backbone of the range and began the descent on the eastern side. But he descended only a short distance before he swung out of the saddle. From the slicker pack on the rear of his saddle he took a pair of heavy leather gloves. He cut these open in the palms with his pocketknife and then tied them about the shoes on his horse's hind feet. The dun was only shod behind.

Again he mounted, and this time he turned to the south and rode down a long slope of lava rock. He grunted with satisfaction, as he looked behind and saw that the leather prevented the shoes on his mount's hind feet from leaving their mark. He was completely obliterating his trail—leaving nothing for the posse to follow, if they should trace him to the top of the range.

He walked his horse slowly, for the dun did not like the idea of the leather tied to its hoofs. In less than two miles the leather was worn through upon the hard rock, and he got down and removed the remnants. He straightened up and looked out over the vista of the desert.

The western sky was a sea of gold. Far to southward a curl of smoke rose upward, marking the course of a railroad and a town. Rathburn looked long in this direction, with a dreamy, wistful light in his eyes. Close at hand vegetation appeared upon the slopes of the hills. His gaze darted here and there along the ridges below him, and his parted lips and eager attitude showed unmistakably that he was familiar with every rod of the locality in which he found himself.

Again he climbed into the saddle and turned off to the left, entering a cañon. For better than half a mile he proceeded down this way, then he rode eastward again, winding in and out in a network of cañons until he came to the rock-ribbed crest of a ridge which overlooked an oasis in the desert hills. There was green vegetation where the water from a spring seeped into the floor of the cañon below him. The spring was nothing more than a huge cup in the rock which had caught the water from the spring rains and filled. Above the spring was a small cabin, and Rathburn saw that the cabin door was open.

Hurriedly he rode down a trail to the right which circled around into the cañon from its lower end. As he galloped toward the spring, a figure appeared in the doorway of the cabin. Rathburn waved an arm and dismounted at the spring. He led his horse to drink, as the man came walking toward him from the cabin. He compelled the dun to drink slowly; first a swallow, now two, then a few more; finally he drew the horse away from the water.

'You can have some more a little later,' he said cheerfully. 'Hello, Joe Price!'

The man walked up to him without a great show of surprise and held out his hand. He was bareheaded, and the hair which hung down to his shoulders was snow-white. The face was seamed and lined, burned by the sun of three score Arizona summers, and the small, blue eyes twinkled.

'Hang me with a busted shoe string if it ain't Rathburn,' said the old man. 'Why, boy, you're just in time for supper. Put your horse up behind the cabin an' get in at the table. She's a big country, all full of cactus; but the old man's got grub left!'

Rathburn laughed, rinsed his mouth out with water he dipped from the spring in a battered tin cup, and took a swallow before he replied.

'Joe, there's two things I want—grub an' gaff. I know you've got grub, or you wouldn't be here; but I don't know if you're any good at the gaff any more.'

The old man scrutinized him. 'You look some older,' he said finally. 'Not much of the wild, galootin' kid left in you, I 'spect. But don't go gettin' fresh with me, or I'll clout you one with my prospectin' pick. Go 'long now; put up your horse an' hustle inside. If you want to wash up, I guess you can—bein' a visitor.'

Rathburn chuckled, as he led his horse around behind the cabin, where two burros were, and unsaddled him. Before he entered the cabin he stood for a moment looking up the ridge down which he had come. The old man watched him, but made no comment. As Rathburn sat down to the table, however, he spoke.

'I kin hear anybody comin' down that trail over the ridge, while they're a mile away,' he said simply without looking up.

Rathburn flashed a look of admiration at the old man.

The glow of the sunset lit the hills with crimson fire, and a light breeze stirred with the advent of the long, colorful desert twilight. They ate in silence, washing down the hardy food with long drafts of strong coffee. The old man asked no questions of his friend. He knew that in time Rathburn would talk. A man's business in that desolate land of dreadful distances was his own, save such of it as he wanted to tell. It was the desert code.

Supper over, they went out to a little bench in front of the cabin. There Joe Price lit his pipe, and Rathburn rolled a cigarette.

For some time they smoked in silence. The purple twilight drifted over the hills, and the breeze freshened in welcome relief to the heat of the day.

'Joe, I just had to come back,' said Rathburn softly. 'Something's wrong with me. You wouldn't think I'd get homesick this way, after all the trouble I've had here, would you?'

The old man removed his pipe. 'Anybody here in particular you want to see?' he asked slowly.

Rathburn shrugged. 'You're always gettin' right down to cases first hand off an' running,' he complained. 'Of course there's folks I want to see. I want to see you, for instance.'

'I don't reckon you'd be ridin' any terrible great distance an' takin' chances by the handful just to see me, boy,' said Price. 'But I ain't tryin' to pry into your affairs. You don't have to answer any of the fool questions I ask you—you know that. I'm an old man an' gettin' childish.'

Rathburn laughed. 'I can believe that when I find you still putterin' around up here where there ain't even a sign of mineral,' he chided.

'There's gold right under your feet,' said the old man stoutly. 'I'll have a payin' vein opened up here in less'n three months.'

'I hope so, Joe. There's nobody I'd like more to see make a big strike than you. You were my dad's friend, an' you've been mine. I haven't got many friends, Joe.'

'But them you've got is good ones,' said Price quickly. 'How long you been away?'

'About eight months,' Rathburn replied with a frown.

'It's hard to get away from the desert,' mused the old man. 'It's in your blood. If you leave here for good you've just naturally got to take something along with you from here—something that's a part of the desert, you might say.'

Rathburn looked keenly at the face of his friend. But the old man was regarding his pipe, as if he had never until that moment seen it.

'I ran into a posse chasin' a gang that robbed a stage on the way over here this noon,' Rathburn said presently.

Price's interest quickened, but he made no sign. 'They saw you?' he asked.

'Couldn't help it,' Rathburn grumbled. 'Took after me. I had to drop one of 'em with a bullet in the shoulder to slow 'em up in the long cañon over on the other side.'

'Know any of the gang?' Price asked.

'Met one. Threw down my gun on him. He told me Mike Eagen was runnin' the works.'

Price nodded. 'I reckon Mike's been pullin' quite a few stunts while you been away.'

'An' I've been gettin' the blame for 'em more'n likely,' said Rathburn in indignation.

Price nodded again. 'Might be so,' he commented.

Rathburn looked up at him in understanding. 'They'll have me mixed up with this stage holdup,' he said earnestly. 'From what I gathered they killed the driver, an' they'll say that was my part.'

'That's the trouble, boy,' said the old miner. 'If a fellow's handy with his gun somebody's sure to get jealous of him an' make him draw. If he gets his man because he has to, he's a killer. When he's known as a killer he ain't got a chance. You *had* to drop the two men you dropped aroun' here, boy; but they ain't forgettin' it.'

'Bob Long was headin' that posse,' said

213

Rathburn thoughtfully.

'An' Bob Long's a sticker when he hits out on a man's trail,' said Price. 'Still, I guess you'd be safe in here for a while. There ain't many knows this place.'

'I don't figure on stayin' here long, Joe,' said Rathburn.

'I didn't think you did,' said Price.

'I'll have to get goin'—hit for new country an' never know when I may run up against the law in a quarter where I ain't expecting it; always sneaking along like the coyote. It was Mike Eagen who gave me that name, Joe.'

Rathburn's voice was low and vibrant, and the old man felt the menacing quality in it.

'What's more,' Rathburn went on, 'I'm always remembering that he's back here, getting away with his dirty tricks, shoving the blame off on me, some way or other, when the chase gets too hot.'

For some time the old man was silent. When he spoke he put an arm about Rathburn's shoulder.

'Boy, before you get worse mixed up than you are, there's a place you ought to visit aroun' here,' he said in a fatherly tone.

Rathburn shrugged and stared up at the night sky which was blossoming with stars.

'It would be a right smart risk,' Price went on, 'for they'd maybe think to drop aroun' that way on a lookout for you; but I reckon before you do much more, you better drop in at the

Mallory place.'

Rathburn rose abruptly. 'I guess that's what I came up here to hear you say,' he said irritably. 'But I don't reckon it can be done, Joe. I haven't any business there.'

'How do you know, boy? Maybe you ain't bein' right fair.'

'Seems to me it would look better for me to stay away.'

'They don't *have* to see you,' urged the old man. 'The Mallory place is a good fifteen miles from Hope, close up against the mountains. Boy, don't you think you better make sure?'

The wistful, yearning look was back in Rathburn's eyes. His right hand rested upon the butt of his gun. The other held his forgotten cigarette. He turned and looked into the old man's eyes.

'Joe, you said something about takin' something from the desert if I left it. You're right. But it can't be, Joe. This thing has killed my chances!'

The gun seemed to leap from its holster into his hand at his hip of its own accord. The old miner's brows lifted in astonishment at the draw.

'If I was you I wouldn't be much scared who I met on the way down to the Mallory place if I didn't meet too many of 'em at once,' he said with a smile.

'I—I couldn't wear it—there,' Rathburn

faltered.

'Well, leave it hangin' on a handy peg, boy,' said the old man cheerfully.

Rathburn jammed the gun back into its holster and walked around to his horse. He led the animal down to drink and then returned and saddled.

'You goin' on tonight?' asked Price casually.

'I'm takin' a ride,' Rathburn confessed.

'You ain't takin' my advice at the same time, are you?' asked Price, pretending to be greatly concerned.

Rathburn mounted and looked down upon him in the faint light of the stars.

'Joe Price, you're a wise old desert rat, an' I'm a young fool,' he said with a twinkle in his gray eyes. 'If Bob Long happens this way give him my regards an' tell him they got the reward notices over in California all right, for I saw 'em stuck up over there. So long.'

The old miner called out after him and watched him ride down the cañon and disappear in the shadows. Nor was he the only watcher; for, high on the ridge above, another man touched his horse with his spurs and started down the west side of the range, as Rathburn vanished.

CHAPTER TWENTY-EIGHT

A NIGHT SUMMONS

In two hours Rathburn came to a fence about a small ranch. Cattle were grazing on the sparse feed within the inclosure, and he saw a clump of trees marking the site of a house.

He rode around the fence until he came to a gate. There was a light shining from two of the windows of the house. He passed through the gate, and, as he approached the house from the side, he saw two figures on the porch. He halted in the shelter of the trees, and, as one of the figures crossed the beam of light which shone out the door, he saw that it was a man. He obtained a fleeting look at the man's face. He was comparatively young, not bad looking, with blue eyes and a small, close-cropped, sandy mustache.

Rathburn scratched his head in an effort to place the man. He seemed vaguely familiar. Rathburn was sure he had seen him somewhere. But he gave up the futile effort to identify him when he saw that the other figure on the porch was that of a girl.

Dismounting, he led his horse around to the rear and put him in a corral near the barn. He surmised that it was about ten o'clock. As he walked toward the front of the house, again he heard the sputtering of a small motor car; then he saw the path of light from its headlights go streaking across the desert in the direction of the town to southward. The front door closed, and all was still.

Rathburn hesitated for several moments, then he stamped up the porch steps and knocked at the door. It was opened by a girl. She held a lighted lamp in her hand. When she saw Rathburn standing, hat in hand, before her, her dark eyes widened, and she nearly dropped the lamp. He stepped forward quickly and took it from her.

'Roger!' she exclaimed breathlessly. 'You—here?'

'I'm here, Laura,' he said quietly. 'I'm home on a—a visit.'

'I heard you were back,' she faltered. 'Mr. Doane—that is—a gentleman from town told me he had heard you were back. But—'

She scanned his face closely and peered beyond him into the shadows with visible concern.

'Roger, come in quickly,' she invited, stepping back from the door.

With a faint smile he entered and closed the door after him. He put the lamp down on the table in what was evidently the sitting room of the small house. He looked about him with the air of one who sees familiar surroundings, but is embarrassed by them.

'Some one been tellin' you the details of my

arrival?' he asked with an effort to appear casual.

'I heard you were in some trouble, Roger.' The girl continued to stare at him with a queer expression in her fine eyes—part sorrow, part concern, part gladness.

'I'm not a stranger to trouble these days, Laura,' he said soberly.

There was a sob in the girl's throat, but she recovered herself at once.

'Have you eaten?' she asked quickly.

'Up at Joe Price's place,' he replied. 'All fed and chipper.'

There was not much confidence in his tone or manner. As the girl lowered her gaze, he looked at her hungrily; his eyes feasted on the coils of dark hair, her long, black lashes, the curve of her cheek and her delicate color, the full, ruby lips, and the small, quivering chin. She was in the throes of a strong emotion.

'I'm sorry, Laura, if—you didn't want me to come,' he said unsteadily.

'Oh, Roger! Of course we want you to come. It's been so long since we saw you. And you've—you've gone through so much.'

She raised her eyes, and the expression which he saw in their depths caused him to look away and to bite his lips.

'There's a lot of it I wish I could undo, Laura; an' there's a lot more of it I couldn't help, an' maybe some I—I—wasn't—' He paused. He couldn't bring himself to say anything in extenuation of himself and his acts in the presence of this girl. It might sound as if he were playing for her sympathy, he thought to himself.

'Roger, I know you haven't done all the things I've heard about,' she said bravely. 'And there's always a chance. You're a man. You can find a way out. If the trails seem all twisted and tangled, you can use a compass—your own conscience, Roger. You still have that.'

'How did you happen to mention the trails bein' all mixed up like that?' he asked curiously.

'Why—I don't know. Isn't that the way it seems?'

Rathburn looked away with a frown. 'You come near hittin' the nail on the head, Laura.'

'Oh, then you *are* beginning to think!' she said eagerly.

'I've done nothing but think for months,' Rathburn confessed.

She looked at him searchingly. Then her eyes dropped to the black butt of the gun in the holster strapped to his right thigh. She shuddered slightly.

'You came from the west, Roger?' she asked.

'Yes,' he replied shortly. 'From where there's water an' timber an' flowers an' grass— but they had my number there, just the same as they've got it here. I'm a marked man,

Laura Mallory.'

She leaned upon the table with one hand; the other she held upon her breast.

'Are—are they—after you, Roger?' she asked in a low, anxious tone.

'As usual,' he answered with a vague laugh. 'Laura, I didn't come here to bother you with my troubles; I come here just to see *you.*'

The girl colored. 'I know, Roger. We've known each other a long time—since we were children. You wouldn't like it for me not to show any concern over your troubles, would you?'

'I wish we could talk about something else,' said Rathburn. 'I can't stay long.'

Laura Mallory looked worried. 'May I ask where you plan to go, Roger?'

'I'm not sure. I only know I wanted to come back, an' I came. I hadn't any fixed plans, an' I wasn't expecting the reception I got.' His face clouded. Then he looked straight into the girl's eyes. 'I hit this country this morning,' he said steadily. 'The first folks I saw was some men ridin' in my direction up between the lava hills and the range. Then things began to happen.'

She nodded brightly. 'I believe you,' she said simply.

Rathburn smiled. 'You always did that, Laura, an' I ain't never been much of a hand at lying.'

'Roger,' she said quickly, 'if they all knew you as well as I think I know you—'

221

'They wouldn't believe,' he interrupted. 'They call me The Coyote, an' they'll have me live up to the name whether I want to or not,' he added bitterly.

'But, Roger, you're forgetting what I said about the trails and the compass.'

'No, Laura, I'm not, but there's another force besides the big lodestone that's affectin' that compass.'

'Roger, you're thinking of an enemy!'

He did not answer her. His face appeared grim, almost haggard, in the yellow rays of the lamplight.

'Roger, you once promised me anything I might ask,' she said softly.

'An' all you have to do is ask,' he answered, taking a step toward her.

'I'm going to ask you for something, Roger,' she said without looking at him. 'Maybe you'll think it's—it's too much that I ask.' She glanced up at him doubtfully.

'What is it, Laura?' he insisted.

'I want your gun, Roger,' she whispered.

He straightened and stared at her in startled wonder. 'But, Laura—a man in my position— why—why—where would I be at?'

'Maybe if you gave it to me it would help you find a way out, Roger,' she pleaded earnestly.

Rathburn looked into her eyes and thrilled. Then without a word he unbuckled his cartridge belt which held his holstered gun, untied the strap about his thigh and laid the belt with the weapon upon the table.

'Roger!' said the girl. The sob again was in her voice. She reached out and placed a hand upon his arm.

An elderly man appeared in the doorway from the kitchen.

'Father, this is Roger,' said the girl hurriedly. 'He's back.'

'What's that? Roger, eh? You mean Rathburn is here?'

The old man peered at the visitor from the doorway, his lean face twitching. He stroked his gray beard in indecision. His blue eyes looked long at Rathburn, then at the girl, and lastly at the gun and belt on the table.

'Well, hello, Rathburn,' he said finally, advancing into the room. He held out a hand which Rathburn grasped.

'Did you eat yet?' asked Mallory.

'In the hills with Joe Price,' replied Rathburn. 'But I'm just as much obliged.'

'Yes, of course,' Mallory muttered. 'With Joe, eh? He ain't been down in months. How is he?'

'Looks good as a gold mine an' thinks he's found one,' said Rathburn, looking at the girl's father curiously.

'That's what keeps him up,' Mallory asserted loudly. 'He'll never get old as long as he thinks he's got a mine corralled. He ought to try stock raisin' for a while. You look older,

Rathburn—more filled out. Are you still cutting 'em high, wide, an' handsome.'

Rathburn's face clouded.

'Roger's starting new, dad,' the girl interposed.

Mallory stared keenly at the younger man. He started to speak, but was interrupted by the sound of horses outside the house.

Rathburn whirled toward the door, took a step, and stopped in his tracks. The girl's hands flew to the sides of her face, and her eyes widened with apprehension.

'I'll go see who it is,' said Mallory with a quick look at Rathburn.

He hastened out into the kitchen, and a moment later they heard the kitchen door open. There was a murmur of voices. The girl stared at Rathburn breathlessly, while he tapped with his slim fingers upon the top of the table.

Then Mallory came in. 'Somebody to see you,' he said to Rathburn.

Rathburn looked once at the white-faced girl and followed her father out into the kitchen. She heard them speak in an undertone, and then Rathburn came back into the room.

'I ain't much elated over my visitor,' he said slowly. 'I wish you hadn't asked me what you did until—well, until this caller had come an' gone.'

She looked straight into his eyes in an agony

of dread.

'Who is it, Roger?' she asked, wetting her lips.

'Mike Eagen is out there,' he answered calmly.

She drew a quick breath, while he waited. Then he turned on his heel and started for the kitchen door.

'Roger!' she called.

He swung about and eyed her questioningly. She pointed at the heavy belt and gun on the table.

'Take it,' she whispered.

He buckled on the belt and tied down the end of the holster so it could not slip if he should draw the weapon within it. Then he made his way into the kitchen and out of the rear door. Laura Mallory sank into a chair, sobbing.

CHAPTER TWENTY-NINE

GUNMEN

For a moment Rathburn waited at the kitchen door. He heard Mallory going upstairs from the next room. All was still outside, save for the stamping of several horses. Then he suddenly opened the door and stepped out. There was no sound or movement, as he accustomed his eyes to the dim light without. He moved across the threshold and walked straight to a bulky figure standing beside a large horse.

'You want to see me, Eagen?' he asked coldly.

'Watch out there, Eagen!' came Mallory's voice in a strident tone from a window above them. 'I've got you covered with this Winchester!'

Both Rathburn and Eagen looked up and saw Mallory leaning out of a window over the kitchen, and the stock of a rifle was snug against his cheek and shoulder.

'Acts like he's scared you can't take care of yourself,' said Eagen with a sneer. 'The way you ditched that posse today I didn't think you needed a bodyguard.'

'I don't,' Rathburn retorted. 'The old man is acting on his own hook. You was watching the sport today?'

'Couldn't help it,' said Eagen. 'It was me an' some of the boys they was after. You sort of helped us out by coming along an' attracting their attention. I pegged you when I saw you ride for it, an' I knew they wouldn't get you.'

'You mean you hid an' let me stand the gaff,' said Rathburn scornfully. 'That's your style, Eagen. You're plumb afraid to come out from under cover.'

He noted that there were three men with Eagen. They were quietly sitting their horses some little distance behind their leader.

Eagen muttered something, and Rathburn could see his face working with rage. Then Eagen's coarse features underwent a change, and he grinned, his teeth flashing white under his small, black mustache.

'Look here, Rathburn, there's no use in you an' me being on the outs,' he said in an undertone. 'We've got something in common.'

'You've made a mistake already,' Rathburn interrupted sharply. 'We haven't a thing in common I know of, Eagen, unless it's a gun apiece.'

'Maybe you think that's all we need,' said Eagen hoarsely; 'an' if that's the way you feel you won't find me backin' down when you start something. Just now I ain't forgetting that crazy fool with that rifle up there.'

'You didn't come here for a gun play, Eagen,' said Rathburn. 'You ain't plumb loco *every* way. I take it you saw me makin' for this place an' followed me here. What do you want?'

'I want to talk business,' said Eagen with a hopeful note in his voice; 'but you won't let me get started.'

'An' I won't have dealings with you,' said Rathburn crisply.

'That's what you think,' sneered Eagen. 'But you're in a tight corner, an' we can help you out. Long said today, I heard just now, that he'd put every deputy he had an' every man he could swear in as a special on your trail, and he'd get you.'

'The thing that I can't see,' drawled Rathburn, 'is what that's got to do with you. I suppose you're here as a missionary to tip me off. Thanks.'

Eagen had calmed down. He stepped closer to Rathburn and spoke in a low tone.

'Here's the lay: They're after you, an' they're after us. I know you're no stool pigeon, an' I know I ain't takin' a chance when I tell you that we've got a big job comin' up—one that'll get us a pretty roll. It takes nerve to pull it off, even though certain things will make it easier. You might just as well be in on it. You can make it a last job an' blow these parts for good. You don't have to come in, of course; but it'll be worth your while. You've got the name, an' you might as well have what goes with it. I'll let you head the outfit an' shoot square all the way.'

Rathburn laughed scornfully. 'When I heard you was out here, Eagen, I guessed it was something like this that brought you here. Maybe you're statin' facts as to this job which, you say, is coming up. But you lied when you said you'd shoot square, Eagen. I wouldn't trust you as far as you could throw a bull by the tail, an' there's half a dozen other reasons why you an' me couldn't be pardners!'

Eagen stepped back with a snarl of rage. 'I don't reckon you're entitled to what rep you've

228

got!' he blurted hoarsely. 'Right down under the skin, Rathburn, I believe you're soft!'

'That's puttin' it up to me all fair an' square,' Rathburn replied evenly. 'I'll give it right back to you, Eagen.'

'Get that gun out of the window.'

'Mallory.'

'Right here, Rathburn, an' all set,' came Mallory's voice.

'Get that gun out of the window.'

'What's that? Don't you see there's three of 'em? You—'

'Get that gun out of the window!' rang Rathburn's voice.

'Let him play with it,' Eagen said harshly.

Mallory withdrew from the window, as Eagen reached for his left stirrup and swung into the saddle.

'I see you ain't takin' it,' Rathburn called to him with a jeering laugh.

'An' I ain't forgettin' it!' Eagen shouted, as he drove in his spurs.

His three companions galloped after him, and Rathburn caught sight of a dark-skinned face, a pair of beady, black eyes, and the long, drooping mustaches of one of the men.

'Gomez!' he exclaimed to himself. 'Eagen's takin' up with the Mexicans.'

Mallory appeared in the kitchen door, holding a lamp above his head. 'What'd he want?' he demanded of Rathburn.

'More'n he got,' answered Rathburn shortly.

229

Then he saw Laura Mallory standing behind her father.

'I mean to say he made a little proposition that I had to turn down,' he amended, with a direct glance at the girl. 'An' now I've got to do some more ridin'.'

'You leavin' tonight?' asked Mallory in surprise. 'We can put you up here, Rathburn, an' I'll keep an eye out for visitors.'

'And we'd have 'em afore mornin',' said Rathburn grimly. 'Eagen will see to it that Bob Long knows I was out here, right pronto. But I aim to stop any posses from botherin' around your place. If there's one thing I don't want to do, Mallory, it's make any trouble for you.'

The girl came walking toward him and touched his arm.

'What are you going to do, Roger?' she asked in an anxious voice.

'I'm goin' straight into Hope,' Rathburn replied.

'But, Roger,' the girl faltered, 'won't that mean—mean—'

'A show-down? Maybe so. I ain't side-steppin' it.'

A world of worry showed in the girl's eyes. 'Roger, why don't you go away?' she asked hesitatingly. 'Things could be worse, and maybe in time they would become better. Folks forget, Roger.'

For a moment Rathburn's hand rested on hers, as he looked down at her.

'There's two ways of forgettin', girlie,' he said soberly. 'An' I don't want 'em to forget me the wrong way.'

'But, Roger, promise me you won't—won't—turn your gun against a man, Roger. It would make things so much worse. It would leave—nothing now. Don't you see? It takes courage to avoid what seems to be the inevitable. That terrible skill which is yours, the trick in this hand on mine, is your worst enemy. Oh, Roger, if you'd never learned to throw a gun!'

'It isn't that,' he told her gently. 'It isn't what you think at all. I'd rather cut off that right hand than have it raised unfairly against a single living thing. They call me a gunman, girlie, an' I reckon I am. But I'm not a killer. There's a difference between the two, an' sometimes I think it's that difference that's makin' all the trouble. I'm still tryin' to steer by that thing you call the compass, an' that's why I've got to go to town.'

He stepped away from her, waved a farewell to Mallory, who was watching the scene with a puzzled expression, and ran for his horse. A minute later the ringing hoofbeats of his mount were dying in the still night.

Laura Mallory swayed, and her father hurried to her with the lamp and put his arm about her.

'What's it all about, sweetie?' he asked complainingly.

'Nothing, daddy, nothing—only I love him.'

A puff of wind blew out the light in the lamp, and father and daughter stood with arms about each other under the dancing stars.

CHAPTER THIRTY

THE SHERIFF'S PLIGHT

Riding slowly Rathburn kept well in toward the range and proceeded cautiously. This wasn't alone a safety measure, for he wished to favor his horse. The dun had been hard ridden in the spurt to gain the mountains ahead of the posse. He had been rested at Price's cabin, to be sure, and also at the Mallory ranch; but now Rathburn had a ride of fifteen miles to the town of Hope, and he did not know how much riding he might have to do next day.

When a scant three miles from Hope, he halted, loosened the saddle cinch, and rested his horse, while he himself reclined on the ground and smoked innumerable cigarettes. He was in a thoughtful mood, serious and somewhat puzzled. The recollection of Eagen's proposition caused him to frown frequently. Then a wistful light would glow in his eyes, and he thought of Laura Mallory. This would be succeeded by another frown, and then his eyes would narrow, and the smile that men had come to fear would tremble on his lips.

He was again in the saddle with the first faint glimmer of the approaching dawn. He covered the distance into Hope at a swinging lope and rode in behind a row of neat, yellow-brick buildings which formed the east side of one block on the short main street.

Securing his horse behind a building midway of the rear of the block, he entered one of the buildings through a back door. It proved to be a combination pool room and soft-drink bar. No one was in the place except the porter who was cleaning up. Rathburn noted that the man showed no evidences of knowing him, although this was Rathburn's home town.

'Kind of early, ain't you, boss?' grinned the porter. 'Maybe you're lookin' for something to start the day with.' He winked broadly.

Rathburn nodded and walked over to the bar.

'Just get in?' asked the porter, as he put out a bottle of white liquor and glanced at the dust on Rathburn's clothes.

'Just in,' replied Rathburn, pouring and tossing off one drink. 'Where's everybody? Too early for 'em?'

'Well, it's about an hour too early on the average, unless there's been an all-night game,' replied the porter, putting the bottle away, as his customer declined a second drink. 'But then there ain't very many in town right now. Everybody's out after the reward money.'

Rathburn lifted his brows.

'Say,' exclaimed the porter eagerly, 'you didn't see any men ridin' looselike, when you was coming in, did you?'

Rathburn shook his head. 'What's all this you're tryin' to chirp into my ear?' he asked.

'Well, Bob Long, the sheriff, has got all his deputies out except just the jailer—there ain't anybody much in jail now, anyway—an' all the other men he could pin a star on, lookin' for a gang that held up the stage from Sunshine yesterday mornin', shot the stage driver dead, an' made off with an express package full of money. There's a big reward out for the man that's leadin' the gang. He's called The Coyote. Used to live here. He's a bad one.'

'Sheriff out, too?' Rathburn asked, showing great interest.

'Sure. Come back in early last night an' got more men. They're tryin' to surround Imagination Range, I guess. That's where this Coyote an' his gang are supposed to be hanging out. The sheriff don't care so much for the fellers that's with him, I guess, but he sure does want this Coyote person. He told everybody to let the gang go if they had to, but to get the leader.'

Rathburn looked through the front windows with a quizzical smile on his lips. The sun was shining in the deserted street.

'How many men has the sheriff got?' he inquired casually.

'Most two hundred, I guess. They're scattered all over the range, an' a lot of 'em has hit over on the other side. They think The Coyote crossed the range an' is makin' east.'

'Well, maybe he has, an' maybe he hasn't,' Rathburn observed. 'The best place to hide from a posse is in the middle of it.'

The porter looked at him, then burst into a loud laugh. 'I guess you said something that time, pardner. In the middle of it, eh?' He went about his work, chuckling, while Rathburn walked to a front window and stood looking out.

A few minutes later he stepped quickly back into a corner, as a small automobile raced up the street. He sauntered to the rear door, passed out with a pleasant word to the porter, and when he gained the open, hurried up behind the buildings the length of the block. There he turned to the left and walked rapidly to a large stone building. He went around on the east side and entered a door on the ground floor. He found himself in a hallway, and on his left was a door, on the glazed glass of the upper half of which was the gold lettering: 'Sheriff's Office.'

After a moment's hesitation he opened the door quickly and went in. A man standing before an open roll-top desk turned and regarded the early-morning visitor. He was a small man, but of wiry build. His eyes were gray, and he wore a small brown mustache. He had a firm chin, and his face was well tanned. He was holding a paper in his hands, and the paper remained as steady as a rock in his grasp. His eyes bored straight and unflinchingly into Rathburn's. He showed no surprise, no concern. He made no move toward the pair of guns in the holsters of the belt which reposed on top of his desk. He spoke first.

'Have you come to give yourself up, Rathburn?'

'Hardly that, sheriff,' replied Rathburn cheerfully. 'I arrived in town this morning after most of the population had moved to the desert and the country aroun' Imagination. I didn't think I was goin' to be lucky enough to catch you in till I saw you arrive in that flivver. Are you back for more recruits?'

The sheriff continued to hold the paper without moving.

'When you first started to talk, Rathburn, I thought maybe bravado had brought you here to make a grandstand play,' he said coolly. 'But I see you're not as foolhardy as some might think. I always gave you credit for being clever.'

'Thanks, Sheriff Long,' said Rathburn dryly. 'There's a few preliminaries we've got to get over, so—'

His gun leaped into his hand and instantly

covered the official. He stepped to the end of the desk, reached over and appropriated the belt with the two guns with his left hand. He tossed the belt and weapons to a vacant chair.

'Now, sheriff, I didn't come lookin' for a cell like you hinted; I drifted in for a bit of information.'

'This is headquarters for that article, especially if it's about yourself,' said Long, dropping the paper on his desk and sitting down in the chair before it.

'What all have you got against me?' frowned Rathburn.

'Nothing much,' said the sheriff with biting sarcasm; 'just a few killings, highway robbery, a bank stick-up, two or three gaming houses looted, and a stage holdup. Enough to keep you in the Big House for ninety-nine years and then hang you.'

Rathburn nodded. 'You're sure an ambitious man, sheriff. The killings now—there was White and Moran, that you know about, an' a skunk over in California named Carlisle, that you don't know about, I guess. I couldn't get away from those shootings, sheriff.'

'How about Simpson and Manley?' countered the official scornfully.

'Not on my list,' said Rathburn quickly. 'I heard I was given credit for those affairs, but I wasn't a member of the party where they were snuffed out.'

'If you can make a jury believe that, you're in the clear,' said Long. 'But how about that stage driver yesterday morning?'

Rathburn's face darkened. 'I got in from the west just in time to stumble on that gang of rats,' he flared. 'That's how your men came to see me. The chase happened to come in my direction, that's all.'

'If you can prove that, you're all right again,' the sheriff pointed out. 'The law will go halfway with you, Rathburn.'

'An' I probably wouldn't be able to prove it,' said Rathburn bitterly. 'Those other things—the bank job an' the gamblin' stick-ups—I was younger then, sheriff, an' no one can say that that bank sharp didn't do me dirt.'

'If you can show a good, reasonable doubt in those other cases, Rathburn, I know the court would show leniency if the jury found you guilty on the counts you just mentioned,' said the sheriff earnestly. 'I'm minded to believe you, so far as yesterday's work was concerned. I have an idea or two myself, but I haven't been able to get a good line on my man. He's too tricky. Of course I'm not going to urge you to do anything against your will. I appreciate your position. You're a fugitive, but you have your liberty. Perhaps you can get away clean, though I doubt it. But there's that chance, and you've naturally got to take it into consideration. And you're not *sure* of anything if you go to trial on the charges there are against you. But it would count like sixty in your favor, Rathburn, if you'd give yourself up.'

Rathburn stared at the official speculatively. His thoughts flashed back along the years to the time when he and Laura Mallory had played together as children. He thought of what she had said the night before about the compass. He shifted uneasily on his feet.

'Funny thing, sheriff, but I had some such fool notion,' he confessed.

'It takes nerve, Rathburn, for a man who is wanted to walk in and give up his gun,' said the sheriff quietly.

'I was thinking of something else,' said Rathburn. 'An' I've got to think some more about this that you've sort of put in my head.'

'How much time do you want, Rathburn?' asked Long.

Rathburn scowled. 'Our positions haven't changed,' he said curtly. 'I'm still the man you're lookin' for. I'll have to do my thinkin' on my own hook, I reckon.'

'Just as you say,' Long said gravely. 'Go over what I've told you carefully and don't make any more false moves while you're making up your mind. You wounded one of my men yesterday.'

'I shot high on purpose,' Rathburn pointed out. 'I didn't aim to be corralled just then.'

'I know you did,' was the sheriff's rejoinder. 'I know you could have killed him. I gave you credit for it.'

'You give me credit for quite a few things, sheriff,' said Rathburn whimsically. 'An' now you'll have to give me credit for bein' plumb cautious. It ain't my intention to have my thinking spell disturbed.'

His gun flashed in his hand.

'I'll have to ask you to go inside an' occupy one of your own cells, sheriff, while I'm wanderin' around an' debatin' the subject.'

'I know you too well, Rathburn,' said the sheriff with a grim smile. 'I'm not armed, and I don't intend to obey you. If you intend to shoot you might just as well start!'

Rathburn gazed at him coolly for a moment; then he shoved his gun in its holster and leaped.

Quick as he was, Long was quicker. The sheriff was out of his chair in a twinkling, and he made a flying tackle, grasping Rathburn about the legs. The two fell to the floor and rolled over and over in their struggles.

Although Rathburn was the larger man, the sheriff seemed made of steel wire. He twisted out of Rathburn's holds, one after another. In one great effort he freed himself and leaped to his feet. Rathburn was up instantly. Long drove a straight right that grazed Rathburn's jaw and staggered him, but Rathburn blocked the next blow and succeeded in uppercutting his left to the sheriff's chin.

They went into another clinch, and the

sheriff got the better of the close fighting. Rathburn's face was bleeding, where it had been cut on a leg of the chair, when they were struggling on the floor. The feel of trickling crimson drove him mad. He threw Long off in an amazing burst of strength and then sent his right to the sheriff's jaw with all the force he could put into it.

Long dropped to the floor, and Rathburn raised him and carried him to a door leading into the jail proper. As he drew open the door, he drew his gun and threw it down on the astonished jailer who was dozing in the little office outside the bars.

'Open up!' Rathburn commanded.

The jailer hastened to obey, as he saw the appearance of Rathburn's face and the dangerous look in his eyes.

Rathburn compelled him at the point of his gun to lead the way to a cell in the rear, unlock it, and go inside. Rathburn pushed Long, who was regaining his senses, in after him and took the jailer's keys.

'Tell Long I'm thinkin' over what he told me,' he said to the jailer, as he locked them in.

Then he hurried back to the entrance, locked it, and tossed the keys in through the bars.

He wet his handkerchief with ice water from a tank in Long's office, wiped his face clean, and left the building.

CHAPTER THIRTY-ONE

A NEW COUNT

As Rathburn wended his way to an obscure restaurant on a side street of the little town which was the county seat of Mesquite County, his thoughts were busy with what he had learned from the sheriff. He knew the official had been right when he said that it would react in Rathburn's favor if he gave himself up. Some of the counts on which he would be indicted undoubtedly would be quashed; others he might disprove. There was a chance that he might get off lightly; in any event he would have to spend a number of years in prison.

Rathburn looked up at the bright sky. At the end of the street he could see the desert, and far beyond, the blue outlines of the mountains. It seemed to him that the sunshine was brighter on this deadly morning when he struggled with troubled thoughts. Having always lived in the open, liberty meant everything to him.

But constantly his thoughts reverted to Laura Mallory. What did she expect of him? What would she think if he were to give himself up? Her talk of the compass—his conscience—bothered him. Why should she

242

say such a thing if she didn't feel more than a friendly interest in him? Did she care for him then?

Rathburn laughed mirthlessly, as he entered the eating house. There was no doubt of it—he was a fool. He continued to think, as he ate; by the time he had finished he found himself in a bad mental state. He wiped some moisture from his forehead, as he left the restaurant. For a moment he felt panicky. He was wavering!

The tenor of his thoughts caused him to abandon his caution. He turned the corner by the State Bank of Hope and walked boldly down the street. Few pedestrians were about. None took any special notice of him, and none recognized him. He turned in at the resort he had visited when he first arrived that morning.

He started, as he entered the place. A deep frown gathered on his face. Gomez, Eagen's Mexican henchman, was at the bar. At first Rathburn feigned ignorance of the Mexican's presence; but Gomez smiled at him, his white teeth glistening against his swarthy skin.

Rathburn marveled at the audacity of the Mexican, who undoubtedly was one of those who had held up the stage the day before, in coming boldly into town. Then he recollected that the sheriff had mentioned he had an idea of who was responsible for that job, but had been unable to get a line on his man. Eagen and his gang were evidently well covered up. If such were the case, Eagen himself might be in town.

It was because he thought he might learn something from Gomez that he finally acknowledged the fellow's greeting by a nod.

The Mexican left the bar and walked up to him. 'We are not afraid to come in town, Mr. Coyote,' he murmured.

'Drop that name,' said Rathburn sharply in an undertone. 'Is Eagen here?'

'He is here,' replied Gomez with another display of his white teeth. 'You want to see him? He is up talking with Mr. Doane.'

Doane! Rathburn remembered the name instantly as being the same which had been spoken by Laura Mallory the night before. He remembered, too, the man who had been there and who had driven away to town in the little car. He surmised that this man had been Doane; and it had been he who had brought the information of Rathburn's arrival and the posse's pursuit to the girl.

'You want to see him?' asked Gomez craftily.

Rathburn had a consuming aversion for the wily Mexican. He hated the shifty look in his eyes and his oily tongue.

'Not yet,' he answered shortly.

'He will be here maybe,' said Gomez eagerly. 'It is you change your mind?'

Rathburn scowled. The Mexican then knew all about the proposition Eagen had made to

244

him the night before. Perhaps he could get more information from him than he had suspected.

'What job is it Eagen is planning?' he asked in a low voice.

There were several men at the bar now, and both Rathburn and the Mexican were keeping an eye upon them.

'Oh, that he will have to tell you himself when you are ready,' Gomez replied.

Rathburn snorted in keen disgust. But Gomez sidled up to him.

'You go to the Mallory rancho last night,' he whispered. 'You are not the only one there last night.' His smile flashed again, as Rathburn looked at him quickly.

'There was another there before,' he continued; 'Mr. Doane. He goes there, too. You have been away a long time, and Mr. Doane take the advantage.'

Rathburn's eyes were narrowing, and the Mexican evidently took his face for an encouraging sign.

'Mr. Doane—he is not lucky at cards,' continued Gomez. 'He like to play, and he play lots; but not too well. Maybe he have more luck in love—while you are away.'

'What do you mean?' asked Rathburn through his teeth.

'Oh, you do not know?' The Mexican raised his black brows. 'While you are away, Mr. Doane make hay while the sun shine bright.

He was there much. He was there last night before you. He tries hard to steal your señorita before you come, and he will try to keep her now.' He winked slyly.

Rathburn suddenly grasped him by the throat. 'What are you tryin' to say?' he asked sternly, shaking the Mexican like a rat.

Gomez broke away, his black eyes darting fire. 'You are a fool!' he exclaimed. 'You get nothing. Even your woman, she is stole right under your eyes. Doane, he goes there, and he gets her. She fall for him fast. Then she talks to you with sugar in her mouth, and you believe. Bah! You think the Señorita Mallory—'

Rathburn's open palm crashed against the Mexican's mouth.

'Don't speak her name, you greaser!'

Gomez staggered back under the force of the slap. His eyes were pin points of fire. He raised his right hand to his mouth and then to the brim of his sombrero. His breath came in hissing gasps, as the hatred blazed in his glittering eyes.

Rathburn's face was white under its heavy coating of tan. He saw the few men at the bar turn and look in their direction, and he realized instinctively that these men were gamblers and shady characters who were probably friends of Eagen and his gang.

'I give you my regards,' cried Gomez in a frenzy of rage. 'You—gringo!'

His right hand tipped his sombrero in a lightning move, and there was a flash in the sunlight filtering through the back windows, as Rathburn's gun barked at his hip.

Gomez crumpled backward to the floor, as the knife dropped from his ˙ grasp at the beginning of the throw.

Rathburn, still holding his smoking gun ready, walked rapidly past the men at the bar and gained the open through the door at the rear.

CHAPTER THIRTY-TWO

THE COMPASS FAILS

In the alley behind the buildings fronting on the main street, Rathburn paused in indecision, while he shoved his gun into the holster on his thigh. He had known by the look in Gomez's eyes that he was going to throw a knife. Instinct had caused him to watch the Mexican's right hand, and, in the instant when Gomez had secured the knife from his hat and snapped back his hand for the throw, Rathburn had drawn and fired. He knew well the dexterity of a man of Gomez's stamp with a knife. The gun route was the only chance to protect his life. But Rathburn realized, too, that he had shot to kill!

He had been incensed by the Mexican's subtle insinuations—maddened by the way he leered when he spoke Laura Mallory's name. He had virtually been driven to it. Even now he could not see how he could have avoided it.

Securing his horse, Rathburn rode swiftly around a back street to a small barn on the edge of the desert. He ordered his mount watered and fed. He had known the man who owned this barn, but the individual who attended to his horse was a new employee. He sat in the little front office which also served as the quarters of the night man, while his horse was being looked after. He had not removed his saddle.

Rathburn's thoughts dwelt on what Gomez had said. There was no question but that the Mexican had taken liberties in saying what he did, but there was more than a glimmer of truth in his statements. Rathburn had seen the man leaving Laura Mallory on the porch of the Mallory ranch house. She had mentioned a man named Doane as having brought word that he, Rathburn, was back in the country and in more trouble. Now Gomez had identified this visitor as Doane, the man who had been calling on Laura Mallory regularly. Rathburn's brows wrinkled at the thought. But why not? What hold had he upon her? It certainly wasn't within his rights to resent the fact that another man had found the girl attractive. But, to his increasing torment, he found that he *did* resent it; he couldn't help it!

Suddenly he remembered that Gomez had said Eagen was paying a call on Doane. What could Eagen have to do with Doane which would warrant his visiting him early in the morning? Rathburn recalled that Gomez had intimated that Doane liked to play cards. Was the man then a professional gambler? But no, Gomez had said he did not play well.

Rathburn tried to recollect where he had seen this man Doane before. The blond face and mustache were vaguely familiar. Again he strove to place the man without result.

He shrugged his shoulders, drew out his gun, and replaced the empty shell with a fresh cartridge. He dropped the weapon back into his holster and went outside to see about his horse. The dun still was feeding. Rathburn contented himself with looking over his saddle and readjusting the small slicker pack on its rear. Then he paced the length of the barn, frowning in a thoughtful mood.

There was only one thing he was reasonably sure of; no one around the town knew that he was the outlaw known as The Coyote. He had not seen anybody he knew except the sheriff, and that official was safely out of the way for the present. Gomez had mentioned his name when they had first met, but he had not been heard save by Rathburn. Therefore, if they were looking for the man who had shot down Gomez, they were merely looking for a man measuring up to his description; and Rathburn doubted if anything would be done until the authorities had been notified. Visitors to the sheriff's office would find Long out and would assume that he had not returned from the chase in the hills. It might be another hour before the sheriff's predicament was discovered. And in that hour—

Rathburn caught himself up with another shrug. He was falling a prey to his former hopeless trend of thought. Resentment was swelling within him again, and he struggled to put it down. Perhaps it would be safer to yield to the inclination to take a chance on the courts.

It was after nine o'clock when he rode out of the barn. He proceeded straight toward the main street of the town. He was struggling with a half-formed resolve; summoning courage by shutting out all recollections save that of Laura Mallory's apparently earnest remark about the compass.

Reaching the main street, he started to turn the corner at the bank building when he suddenly checked his horse and stared at two people walking up the opposite side of the street. Rathburn recognized the girl immediately. She was Laura Mallory. A moment later he caught a glimpse of the man's face, as he half turned toward Rathburn, laughing. He had taken Laura's arm. It was Doane!

The realization that Laura had come to town and was in the company of Doane stunned Rathburn. More than anything else it had the effect of convincing him that Gomez had been right when he had hinted that Doane was successful in love. Hadn't she told him to take his gun when Eagen had been waiting for him? Had she thought, perhaps, that there would be gun play, and that Eagen might emerge the victor, thus assuring her that he, Rathburn, would bother her no more?

Rathburn's eyes narrowed, and his face froze, as he watched Laura and Doane out of sight up the street. He knew now why he had had to come back. There was nothing left—nothing but his dreams, his sinister reputation, and his gun!

He looked about in a different way from that in which he had first surveyed the street, now showing life. His gaze encountered the bank building. The door was open. The bank doubtless opened at nine o'clock. He remembered that this was so. A second of indecision, then he moved in front of the bank. He dismounted, flung the reins over the dun's head, and entered briskly.

Two men were behind the screens of the two cages. Rathburn approached a window and nodded to the man behind it. Then his gun leaped into his hand, and he covered the pair.

'Reach high an' hard!' he commanded. 'An'

quick!'

The men in the cages hesitated; but the look in Rathburn's eyes convinced them, and they raised their hands over their heads. Rathburn leaped to the ledge outside the window and climbed nimbly over the wire network of the cage. Then he dropped to the floor inside.

CHAPTER THIRTY-THREE

FAST WORK

Quickly and methodically Rathburn went about his work. His face was drawn and pale, but his eyes glittered with a deadly earnestness which was not lost upon the two men who obeyed his orders without question. The very boldness of his intrepid undertaking must have convinced them that here was no common bandit. He herded them back toward the vault at the point of his gun. Then he ordered them into the vault.

'Now then,' he said crisply, 'you know what I'm after. Trot it out!'

One of the men, evidently an assistant cashier or head teller, who was in charge, opened a compartment of the inner safe and pulled out a drawer. Rathburn could see the packages of bills. He looked quickly about and saw a pile of empty coin sacks on a shelf.

'Fill two of those large sacks,' he instructed the other man.

The clerk hastened to carry out his orders and jammed package after package of bills into one of the largest of the coin sacks. Both men were white-faced and frightened. They did not try to delay the proceedings. Rathburn looked dangerous; and what was more sinister, he went about his nefarious business in a cool, calm, confident manner. He did not look like the Rathburn who had visited Laura Mallory the night before, nor the Rathburn who had talked with the sheriff. In this critical moment he was in look, mood, and gesture The Coyote at his worst—worthy of all the terrible things that had been whispered about him.

It may be that the bank employees suspected as much. It may be that they didn't believe it would be possible for the outlaw to make his getaway in broad daylight, and it was certain that they stood in mighty fear of him. They cowered back, pale and shaking, as he calmly took the sack, heavy with its weight of bank notes of healthy denomination, and stepped to the entrance to the big vault.

'When they come an' let you out,' said Rathburn, 'you can tell them that the gent who helped himself to the berries in the cash box is just beginnin' to cash in on the reputation that's been wished on him!'

He smiled grimly, as he swung the light, inner door of the vault shut and clamped down the lever. He slid his gun into its holster and, carrying the sack of loot, walked out of the door of the second cage toward the main entrance of the bank. As he reached the door, a man came up the steps. Rathburn recognized Doane, and his lips curled in a snarl. It was the first time Doane had come face to face with him, but the man started back in surprise.

'Rathburn!' he exclaimed.

Rathburn hesitated. His first feeling of instinctive animosity fled. He scowled in a swift effort to place the man, and the thought that in an indirect way Doane was partly responsible for what had come to pass flashed through his tortured brain. This brought swift comprehension of his immediate danger. Now that he had taken the decisive step he would have to call upon all his resources of courage and cunning to protect his liberty. The die had been cast!

He hurried past Doane, swung into the saddle, and rode at a swift pace around the corner, leaving Doane standing on the steps of the bank, staring after him with an expression of amazement on his face.

Rathburn knew it would be but a matter of a very few minutes before the knowledge that the State Bank of Hope had been held up and robbed—would be common property in the town. The very boldness of the robbery had insured its success, for none would dream that a lone bandit would have the nerve to come into town in broad daylight, hold up the bank, and attempt to run for it across the open, burning spaces of the desert. But he was not aware of the coincidence which would make the news of the robbery known sooner than he expected.

At the end of the side street he struck boldly across the desert, driving in his spurs and urging the gallant dun to its top speed. In a matter of minutes he was out of view of the town—a speck bobbing amid the clumps of mesquite, palo verde, and cactus. He raced for the mountains in the northwest.

There was another element of uncertainty which entered into the probability of quick pursuit, as he had shrewdly divined. It might be some time before the sheriff's predicament was discovered. Meanwhile most of the male population was scouring the vicinity of Imagination Range looking for him, and there would be no one to lead a second posse until the sheriff was liberated. There was nothing in sight behind him toward town except the vista of dry desert vegetation swimming in the heat. Rathburn rode on with a feeling of security, so far as trouble from that quarter was concerned.

His thoughts were in a turmoil, and he passed a shaking hand over his damp brow. The resentment had given way to grim decision and determination. Well, he had shown them what The Coyote could do. They

255

would remember that job; they could lay that at his door. The proceeds would carry him a long way. They had given him his reputation, and he would make the game worth the candle!

The old fierce defiance of misguided youth was in his veins. He felt a wild exultation seize him. Doubt and all problems were set aside. His eyes glowed with a reckless light, as he raced on toward the blue hills.

Doane had known him—had called him by name. Therefore Doane knew he was The Coyote—the outlaw with a price on his head. So much the better. He *wanted* them to know!

The sun was at its zenith, as he passed above the Mallory place. He did not once turn his head and look down upon it. His jaw was squared, his lips pressed tight, as he guided his horse into the winding foothills of the range. In a narrow cañon he dismounted and undid his slicker pack. When he again tied it behind the saddle it contained the bag which held the bank notes he had taken that morning. He pushed on in the early afternoon.

He now rode with more caution. The fact that he had not seen any members of the posses which were scouring the hills, he accredited to ignorance on their part of the fact that he had been at the Mallory ranch the night before and had gone into town. These things they had hardly had time to learn. More than likely they had assumed that he had crossed the mountains, and it was possible that most of the men on the hunt were on the east side of the range. He became more and more convinced of this as the afternoon wore on, but he did not relax his vigilance. His face had clouded.

'We made a mistake, hoss,' he muttered, 'in not remembering to hunt up Mike Eagen first thing.'

In the quick moves following his sudden momentous decision, he had forgotten Eagen. This fact now bothered him. He had a score to settle with Eagen on general principles. This did not mean that he necessarily would have to shoot Eagen down; but he wanted Eagen to hear straight out what he thought of him. It might be a long time before he could gratify that desire after the events of this day.

Slowly he proceeded, not once venturing upon a high spot until he had investigated by crawling to a vantage point on his hands and knees. It was sundown when he saw the first riders. Two were farther down the slopes to westward, and several more were far to eastward. It was true then that Long had thrown a cordon about the section of the mountains which he had been seen to enter the day before.

However, Rathburn's knowledge of the range and the secrets of the mountain trails gave him a distinct advantage over the inexperienced members of the posses. True, there were deputies and some others who were experienced; but they were in the minority.

Rathburn realized that the sheriff must have been released some hours before, and that his escapade of the morning would stimulate the man hunt. The rewards would be increased, and every able-bodied man in Hope would doubtless join in the scramble for the reward money. He was satisfied that Sheriff Long's order would be to 'shoot on sight!'

On the very crest of the range he paused in the shelter of the rocks. There still was a fair chance for him to get away clean to eastward. The sheriff had not had time to get more men over there, and by making a break into the southeast and then cutting straight to the east, there was a strong possibility that he would succeed in circling around the posse and effect his escape.

But something was drawing him to Joe Price! He did not quite understand that it was the desire to confide in and confess to his friend what had actuated his choice of moral trails. But the yearning was there, and he was yielding to it. He conjectured shrewdly that Long might not dream that he would have the temerity again to enter the very district where he was being sought. It was his belief that the best place to hide from a posse was in the midst of it!

It was this confidence, almost as much as his skill in trailing, which enabled him to gain a point above Joe Price's cabin in the early twilight. He waited patiently until the curtain of night had fallen, and the stars had replaced the fading banners of the sunset, before he slipped down a steep slope and walked his horse into the cañon below the old miner's abode.

CHAPTER THIRTY-FOUR

THE COMPASS WAVERS

Joe Price regarded Rathburn with a curious look in his eyes when he beheld him in the doorway of his cabin. He stepped swiftly to the one window, which was over the table, and dropped the burlap shade. Then he closed the door.

'So they've been here?' asked Rathburn.

'What else could you expect?' replied Price testily. 'They're combin' these hills for you.' He looked at Rathburn keenly, but Rathburn only smiled.

'That's not news to me,' he said quietly; 'I've percolated through their lines twice.'

'Stay here,' said Price, 'and I'll look after your horse—or were you hidin' up all day?'

'No such luck,' answered Rathburn grimly.

The old man looked at him curiously; then he went out of the door, closing it carefully after him.

Rathburn found cold food, put it on the table. and sat down to eat. When Price returned he had finished. The old miner sat down in a chair opposite Rathburn.

'Now, out with it,' he said. 'Something has happened. I can see it in the way you look an' act. What's up?'

Rathburn carefully rolled a brown-paper cigarette, snapped a match into flame, and lit it before he replied. He was half smiling.

'I held up the State Bank of Hope this mornin' an' extracted a bag of perfectedly good bills,' he announced. 'Didn't bother with the counter money. Made 'em serve me from the vault.'

Joe Price's eyelids did not even flicker.

'Any idea what you got?' he asked.

'Not whatsoever,' replied Rathburn coolly; 'but the smallest I saw on top of the package was a fifty.' Price nodded. 'You got plenty,' he said.

Rathburn scowled. He had expected some kind of an outbreak—at least a remonstrance from his old friend. He glanced about uneasily and then glared defiance at Price.

'It had to come, Joe,' he asserted. 'There wasn't any way out of it. What's more, I killed that greased pard of Eagen's, Gomez.'

'How so?' queried Price.

'Well, I'll tell *you*, Joe, but I don't expect it to go any further. He said something about

Laura Mallory an' a man named Doane, an' I didn't like it. I slapped him. Then he went for a knife he had in his hat.'

The old man nodded again. 'I see,' he said simply. 'You shot him. Not a bad riddance. How did you come to rob the bank, Rathburn?'

Rathburn's gaze again shifted uneasily. Then he rose with a burning look at Price, walked up and down the slanting length of the cabin, and halted before the old miner.

'Joe,' he said in a tremulous voice, 'it's the last ditch. I can't get away from it. I thought I could tell you—an old friend—the whole story, but I can't, Joe. That's the devil of it! There's something wrong with me. I reckon I'm one of those fellows who just had everything mapped out for him. I had some trouble, Joe, an' it's started something—something I can't control. They *had* to remember me, an' I gave them something to remember me by!'

'Who do you mean by "they," Rathburn?' asked the miner.

'Sheriff Long an' the others,' said Rathburn quickly. 'There wasn't a chance for me. Why, I was thinking of giving myself up only this morning. Joe, it ain't in the pictures—not after I let Gomez have it. Even after I stopped Gomez I had an idea that I could face the music. Besides, Joe, there's more to this than you think. They call me The Coyote, an', Joe, so help me, from now on I am!'

'Did you stop at the Mallory place?' asked Price quietly.

Rathburn did not reply at once. With agony in his eyes he looked at his old friend, and suddenly he bristled:

'I might as well never have gone there,' he flung out. 'I see now I wasn't wanted. I found out as much from Gomez. He told me about Laura's affair with that fellow Doane. But what could I expect? I wasn't entitled to no thought from her, an' I should have known as much. I'm just a plain fool—a worse one now than I was before.'

Joe Price's faded blue eyes glowed with comprehension.

'You thought Laura had put you off, so you gave in an' robbed the bank, Rathburn, an' just naturally made a mess of things when you had a chance,' said the old man stoutly. 'That ain't actin' with a lick of sense. You wasn't gettin' square with anybody, an' you wasn't doin' that girl right by takin' the word of Gomez.'

'I saw the two of them, her an' Doane, in Hope this morning, walkin' down the street, arm in arm, laughing—probably over me,' Rathburn replied bitterly. 'I've got eyes, and I can put two an' two together. I'm only The Coyote with her, and I'll *be* The Coyote. She took my gun an' then gave it back when Mike Eagen showed up, thinkin' maybe there'd be gun play, an' I'd get mine.'

'Now you shet up!' shrilled Price. 'I reckon

you've lost all the brains you ever did have! Do you think Laura would keep your gun, knowin' there might be trouble, an' you wouldn't have any way to protect yourself? Don't you suppose she knows you're as fast as Eagen? She's no fool, if you are. But, if you've got to stay the fool, you better be lightin' out with your winnings. An' you're not takin' the bank's money, either.'

'What do you mean by that?' scowled Rathburn, who had been thoughtful while his friend was speaking.

'I had money in that bank, Rathburn, an' so did Mallory, an' there's a lot more of us—'

'I'll give you back your money,' Rathburn growled. 'Anyway, they're protected by insurance, an' the insurance people can hunt me till doomsday—I guess.' He was cooling off rapidly.

'Maybe they are,' said Price, 'an' maybe they ain't. But it ain't goin' to help you none the way you're goin' to feel about it later, no matter who loses it.'

Rathburn was pacing the room, frowning. Twice he started to speak, but the words failed to come. Then he put a question. 'Who is this man Doane? He knew me, for I met him when I was comin' out of the bank, an' he called me by name.'

'Doane is cashier of the bank down at Hope. He was likely just comin' to work when you met him.'

Rathburn stared with an incredulous expression. 'You're sure?' But even as he put the question, Rathburn placed his man.

'I'm dead certain on it,' declared Price.

Rathburn sat down heavily and took his hat in his hand.

'That makes it different,' he said dully, as if to himself. 'Maybe she's stuck on him for his money, an' maybe she's stuck on him because he's a good guy. Maybe this thing would hurt him.'

'Oh, I don't think they'd blame him,' said Price with a note of consolation in his voice; 'an' he probably wouldn't lose nothin'.'

'But she might think—it might be that she—' Rathburn swung his hat to his head and rose. He walked toward the door, but Joe Price got in his way.

'Where you goin'?' he asked.

'To the Mallory ranch!'

'You can't get there!' said Price hoarsely, pushing him back.

'I've got to get there!' answered Rathburn grimly, pushing the old man aside. 'I must see Laura.'

'You got here just by luck,' Price pointed out. 'An' there's more men in by now. Maybe they know you're here. But wait till I get your horse—he's hid.'

'Get him,' Rathburn commanded.

After a moment's hesitation Price went out the door, and he returned almost instantly. He walked to the table and blew out the light. 'Go to the door an' see,' he urged in an excited voice.

Rathburn hurried out. High on the mountain above the cañon a fire was burning.

'It's the signal,' Price whispered in his ear.

'Joe, do me a last favor,' said Rathburn in a queer voice. 'Get me my hoss before it's too late!'

The old man obediently slipped into the shadows behind the cabin.

CHAPTER THIRTY-FIVE

GUNS IN THE NIGHT

When Joe Price returned, leading Rathburn's horse which he had fed and watered, and turned over the reins, he spoke swiftly in a low voice:

'They'll be watchin' hard for you down the cañon, boy. Bob Long's sure to mean business this 'ere time.'

'Well, I know it,' said Rathburn with a low, mirthless laugh. 'I locked him in his own jail this mornin' to get a clean chance to decide to give myself up. Then, when the chance came— well, he surely thinks now that I put him away to cover my tracks. I expect the boys have got their shootin' orders.'

'Listen!' whispered Price excitedly. 'Wait till I get my own horse, an' I'll strike east across the hump. That'll start 'em after me maybe—sure it will, Rathburn! They'll think I'm you, see, an' light right out after me.'

Rathburn laid one hand on the old man's shoulder and put the other over Joe's mouth.

'Joe, you're all excited—plumb unreasonable excited. You know I wouldn't let you do that. Now don't hand me more worries than I've got. Be good, Joe.' He patted Price's shoulder, then swung into the saddle.

The old miner looked up at him, his face showing strangely white in the dim starlight, pierced by the fire on the peak.

'I didn't tell 'em you'd been here, Roger; don't forget that!'

'I knew that, Joe,' Rathburn chuckled. 'So long.'

Swiftly he rode down the little meadow below the spring into the deep shadows of the cañon which led down a steep trail to the desert. Presently he checked his pace until he was walking the gallant dun. He wished to avoid as much noise as possible, and to save the horse for a final spurt down nine miles of desert to the Mallory ranch from the mouth of the cañon—providing he got out.

For two reasons he had deliberately chosen this route: it was shortest, and it offered the best going. He must save the dun's strength. Rathburn knew the limits of his splendid mount; knew they had almost been reached; knew there was just enough left in the horse to make the ranch without killing him. The Coyote would surrender before he would kill his horse to effect his escape or gain an objective!

Thus they slipped down the narrow cañon, with the desert stars gleaming white above the lava hills of Imagination Range, while the fire glowed on the peak above Joe Price's cabin. Rathburn's face was pale under his tan; his thoughts were in a turmoil, but his lips were pressed into a fine line that denoted an unwavering determination. Had Sheriff Bob Long seen his face at this time he might have glimpsed another angle of Rathburn's many-sided character—an angle which would have given him pause.

Rathburn looked behind, and his eyes narrowed. Two fires were burning on the peak.

Already the watchers were cognizant of his latest move and were signaling to those who might be below. He wondered vaguely why they had not surrounded Joe Price's cabin while he had been there. Then he realized he had been there hardly long enough for his pursuers to get there in any number. Suddenly his thoughts were broken into by a streak of red in the cañon depths below him. He swerved close against the rock wall, drew his gun, and, speaking to the dun, drove in his spurs.

A short distance below he could see the faint glow of the starlight night and knew he was near the cañon's mouth. There were more streaks of red, and bullets whistled past him. Then Rathburn raised his gun and sent half its deadly contents crashing down into the trail ahead.

There followed a few moments of quiet, broken only by the harsh, ringing pound of his mount's hoofs. Rathburn could see open country just ahead. Then a flash of fire came from almost under him, and the big dun lunged into the air, half twisting, and came down upon some object under its hoofs. The dun bounded on in great leaps, literally flying through the air, as Rathburn thrilled with the knowledge that the horse had knocked down the man who had sought to kill him.

From above came sharp reports, and the blackness of the high cañon walls was streaked with spurts of flame. Leaden death hurled itself into the rock trail behind him. Then he was out of the cañon, riding like mad through the white desert night toward his goal—the Mallory ranch!

*　　　*　　　*

Laura Mallory stood on the porch of the little ranch house, staring out across the dimly lit spaces of desert. A worried look appeared in her eyes. The front door was open, and in the small sitting room her father was reading under a shaded lamp at the table. At times the worried look in the girl's eyes would change to one of wistfulness, and twice the tears welled.

Presently she straightened and listened intently, looking into the south instead of northwest. Her ears, keen as are those of the desert born, had caught a sound—a succession of faint sounds—in the still night air. Gradually the sound became more and more distinct, and the worried expression of her face increased. She hurried into the sitting room.

'Father, Fred Doane is coming out from town,' she said breathlessly. 'Do you suppose they've got him?'

'Maybe so, girlie,' said the old man. 'It was a bold business, an' what could you expect?'

'Oh, I don't know. I can't seem to understand. All this trouble is coming so suddenly. Father, are you sure you heard Roger refuse to aid that man Eagen in some shady scheme last night?'

'Ab-so-lutely,' declared Mallory. 'I've been wondering, daughter, if he didn't turn Eagen down because he had this scheme of his own.'

The purr of a motor came to them from outside, and Laura, hastily wiping her eyes with a small handkerchief, went slowly out.

'Laura!' cried Fred Doane, as he came up the steps, holding out his hands.

'What—what is it, Fred?' she faltered. 'Have they caught—'

269

'Not yet,' said Doane briskly, as Mallory appeared in the door. 'An' they probably won't get him. He's clever, that fellow.'

The bank cashier indulged in a frown, but he was plainly nervous.

'Then what news do you bring here?' Mallory demanded. 'Did you come to tell us he'd got away clean?'

'Why, not—not exactly,' said Doane. 'I meant to tell you that, of course, but I also want to have a little talk with Laura. Can I see you alone, Laura, for a few minutes?'

'Oh, *that's* it,' snorted Mallory, as he stamped back into the house.

'You have something to tell me you don't want father to hear?' asked the girl in a worried voice.

'Laura, there's something I must tell you right away,' said Doane nervously, leading her to the shadow of the far end of the porch. There he turned and faced her, taking her hands.

'Laura, you must have seen it for a long time. You could hardly help but see it. I love you, Laura—I love you with all my heart, and I want you to be my wife.'

The girl drew back in astonishment.

'But why do you have to tell me this so suddenly?' she asked, her color coming and going.

'Because I want you to marry me, Laura, tonight!' he said. Again he reached for her hands. 'Please, Laura,' he pleaded. 'It means so much to me. Don't you care for me, sweetheart? I've been led to think you did, and 1 intended to tell you soon, but all this trouble—this terrible trouble today—has nearly driven me mad. I'm afraid I'll go mad, Laura, if I don't have something else to think about. Oh, Laura, marry me and help me out of this big trouble.'

'Fred!' exclaimed the girl, startled by his passion of pleading. 'Fred, I've never tried to make you think I cared for you. And now—well, I'd have to have a long time to think it over. How would it help you out of trouble, Fred? Tell me that.'

'By helping me forget—by helping me forget that our bank is ruined! By saving my mind! By keeping me from going mad! By—'

'Fred you must not talk so. That robbery has unnerved you for the time being, that's all. You're excited and so—'

'I'm more than excited,' he declared, trying to put his hands on her shoulders. 'I'm about—about *gone*! Laura, marry me tonight, and we'll go somewhere—we'll go somewhere right from here, from this ranch—go a long way and get married in the morning. Then we can stay away for a short time till I get to be myself again.'

'No, Fred,' replied the girl in convincing tones, 'I can't. It would be asking too much even if I loved you. Come inside, and I'll make you some strong tea. You can talk to father and me and regain control of yourself.'

There was a moment of silence. Mallory with the lamp had come to the door at the sound of Doane's loud voice. He was looking at them. Then out of the night came the pound of hoofs. There was no mistaking the sound.

Doane whirled around, as a rider came out of the sea of mesquite and greasewood and flung himself from the saddle in front of the porch. The bank cashier turned toward Mallory. His face was haggard. He seemed to sway, as the rider came stamping up the steps. He darted for the door, but had hardly got inside before the rider caught him and made him face about. Mallory hurried in with the lamp, followed by the girl.

Doane was quailing before the new arrival. Both cried out, as they saw it was Eagen who had broken out so suddenly. Eagen towered above the shrinking Doane.

'So you thought you'd double cross me, did you, eh?' came Eagen's harsh voice, and he slapped Doane in the face.

Doane went red, then white. For a moment intense hatred and anger flashed in his eyes, but he made no move to avenge the insult. Slowly the light in his eyes died again to fear, as he realized his inability to cope with this man of strength.

'Here, Eagen, you can't come into my house and act like that,' said Mallory stoutly, putting the lamp on the table.

Laura still stood in the doorway, stunned by the rapid and extraordinary turn of events. Eagen turned on Mallory with a snarl.

'Shut up, you old fool! Don't butt in where you ain't wanted, an' on something you don't know anything about.'

'I know you're in my house!' Mallory retorted sternly.

'I'll only be here a minute,' said Eagen with a sneer. 'I'm goin' out of your house, an' I'm goin' to drag this sneaking cur out with me—out on the solid ground an' give him what's comin' to him. An' then,' he added in a terrible voice; 'I'm goin' to go out an' get his pardner—Rathburn, The Coyote—get him when the others can't come within a mile of him!'

'You can't take this man out of my house when he is my guest!' thundered Mallory.

'No?' asked Eagen contemptuously. 'Well, you watch an' see! If you try to stop me you'll stop lead!'

He leaped forward and grasped Doane by the shoulder, jerked him forward, and stepped backward himself. He turned, dragging his victim, then stopped dead in his tracks with a hissing intake of breath. Rathburn was standing quietly in the doorway.

CHAPTER THIRTY-SIX

THE LOOT

In the heat of the threats and counterthreats which had been in progress, none of the occupants of the room had heard the newest arrival thunder up to the porch and leap from the saddle to the steps.

Eagen was dumfounded by Rathburn's sudden appearance. He saw that the girl was standing now in a front corner of the room, with her hands crossed on her breast, a look of horror in her eyes. Slowly Eagen recovered and loosed his hold on Doane, who staggered weakly to the table and leaned upon it. Eagen's sneer returned to his thick lips, and his narrowed gaze traveled quickly to a sack which Rathburn held in his left hand. Eagen's eyes shone with fury.

'Come here to fix up the divvy!' he choked. 'I knew it was a put-up job between you an' Doane, an' I figured you'd maybe meet aroun' here where Doane would be sure to come to try an' take this woman with him.'

Rathburn eyed him calmly. There was something of a deadly calm in his very posture, as he stood just within the threshold. He looked past Eagen to Doane. Then he tossed the sack on the table.

274

'Here's the money I took this morning, Doane,' he said in matter-of-fact tones. 'I came here to turn it over to you.'

With bulging eyes Doane stared at him.

Eagen laughed loudly. 'That's rich! Tryin' to make me think you was goin' to give it *all* to him? Don't you figure, Mr. Coyote, that I can throw my rope aroun' a simple scheme like you an' that shivering rat over by the table cooked up? That's why you turned down my little proposition last night. It was this same deal—only, *me* an' Doane there was goin' to put it over. You figured I'd cut you out of your divvy, an' you figured right; he suspected I might double cross him, an' maybe he was right, too. So he cooked it up with you to pull the robbery, thinkin' you'd be more likely to go through an' give him his end. But the pair of you figured too many points when you thought I wouldn't catch on.'

'That was what your proposition was to be, was it?' asked Rathburn pleasantly. 'Rob the bank? Why, I didn't need a gang to rob the bank, Eagen, an' I didn't have anybody in with me. The trouble with you is that you've got too much imagination.'

The drawl in which Rathburn concluded his speech drove Eagen to a frenzy.

'You lie, Rathburn!'

Rathburn smiled. 'I might as well tell you that I intended to get away with that money that's on the table, Eagen. That's what I took

275

it for. I'm making this little statement because something's liable to happen to one, or both of us. I didn't know Doane was cashier of the bank when I took it. I only recently learned that fact. Then I brought it back to turn over to him, not so much on his account as on account of Miss Mallory. I understand Doane is a very good friend of Miss Mallory. I wouldn't want his bank hurt for that reason.'

It was Laura Mallory who cried out at this. She walked toward Rathburn, although he did not look at her.

'Why did you do it, Roger?' she asked in a trembling voice.

'I can't tell you *that*, ma'am,' he said.

'But I know!' she cried. 'I've guessed it. You saw Mr. Doane and me together in Hope today and remembered he was at the ranch last night, and—'

'Don't say any more, Laura!' Rathburn commanded sternly.

'Be still, daughter; it's best,' said Mallory.

'Neither she, nor you, nor Doane, nor all of you together can talk me out of it!' roared Eagen. 'It was a frame-up!'

In the deadly stillness that followed, Laura Mallory shrank back from the sight of two gunmen looking steadily into each other's eyes, their hands ready for the lightning draw—each waiting for the merest suggestion of the beginning of a move on the part of the other to get his weapon into action. But the draws did not come. The pregnant silence was broken by the thundering roll of many horses galloping into the yard about the house.

'There!' yelled Eagen in a voice of triumph. 'There's your sweet little posse, Coyote!'

'I expected to see Bob Long when I came down here!' said Rathburn coolly, looking at Laura Mallory for the first time.

CHAPTER THIRTY-SEVEN

THE TEST OF A MAN

Several men stamped across the porch to the jingle of spur chains. Others broke in through the back door and entered the kitchen. Sheriff Bob Long appeared at the door, with two guns leveled.

'You're covered from both doors and all the windows, Rathburn!' he said sharply.

'That's almost just what I thought, sheriff,' Rathburn drawled.

Long stepped into the room, shoving his guns into their holsters. Many other guns were covering Rathburn.

'What's the meaning of all this, anyway?' demanded Long with a puzzled expression on his face. His eyes widened, as he saw the bag of money on the table. 'Is that the money that was taken from your bank this morning Mr.

Doane?' he asked sharply.

Doane nodded weakly. The sheriff looked at Rathburn curiously.

'You brought it back? You was up to Joe Price's place.'

'Yes, I brought it back, sheriff,' said Rathburn cheerfully.

'Well, I'll be frank and tell you, Rathburn, that if you expect leniency after what happened this morning you might just as well give up that idea. Any man can change his mind when he sees he can't get away.'

'That's up to you, sheriff,' replied Rathburn, taking tobacco and papers from his shirt pocket. 'As I was just tellin' our friend, Mr. Eagen, I brought it back on purpose, an' I expected to see you when I got here. I came near not gettin' here at that.'

'You took a long chance,' scowled Long. 'But it won't get you much now at this stage of the game—especially after the way you led me to believe this morning that you were thinking of giving yourself up.'

Eagen's laugh startled them.

'He brought it back to give it up an' himself, too?' he jeered. 'He brought it back, sheriff, because he an' that rat of a Doane planned this thing. Coyote got away with the money an' came back here to divvy up with Doane. Didn't Doane make the same kind of a proposition to me? Didn't he tell me he was short in his accounts, an' it could be covered up if the bank

278

was robbed, for then he could say more money was took than really was? I'll say he did. An' I was goin' to see if he'd go through with it, an' then I was going to wise you up so we could get him cold.'

With knitted brows the sheriff stared at Eagen, then looked at the white-faced Doane.

'Tell him I'm tellin' the truth!' shouted Eagen at the shaking bank cashier. 'You can't get out of it.'

There was a tense moment.

Doane shook his head weakly; he was a picture of guilt.

'He got scared I wouldn't go through with the play, sheriff,' Eagen continued. 'Thought maybe I'd make off with all the kale. So he framed it with Rathburn, an' I caught 'em about to divide it here.'

'He lies!' screamed Doane. 'I didn't frame it with Rathburn. I can prove it. That man'—he pointed a shaking finger at Eagen—'has come to me with threats and made me take securities I knew were stolen. There's some of them in the bank now. Some of the stuff he took from the stage driver yesterday is there! He's pulled job after job—'

Eagen, recovering from his amazement at the man's outbreak, leaped and drove his powerful fist against Doane's jaw, knocking him nearly the length of the room, where he crashed with his head against the stones of the fireplace. Eagen turned quickly. His eyes were

279

blazing red.

'You're the man!' he yelled wrathfully. 'You're the yellow Coyote—'

His right hand went to his gun, as there came a crashing report. He staggered back, trying to get out the weapon which had not left his holster. He sank down to his knees, still glaring death at the man above him, still fumbling at his gun. Then he lurched forward on his face.

Rathburn flipped his smoking pistol so that its barrel landed in his hand. Then he tendered it, butt foremost, to Sheriff Bob Long. Long took it and threw it on the table, looking first at Rathburn, then at the dead man on the floor. He waved toward the doors and windows.

'You boys can draw back,' he ordered.

Mallory stepped to the fallen Doane. The man's face had set in a white cast. He felt his heart.

'He did for him,' he said, rising.

Laura Mallory came walking slowly up to the sheriff. Her face was ghastly after what she had witnessed.

'Sheriff Long,' she said in a voice strangely calm, 'we heard Eagen'—she shuddered, as she mentioned the name—'ask Roger—ask Mr. Rathburn last night to help with some job that would get them a lot of money. It may be that—that—Fred *did* plan such a thing. I'm sorry to say it, but Fred had seemed awfully nervous lately, and tonight he came to me and asked me to run away with him—at once. He seemed horribly afraid of something. Anyway, Roger refused to go in with Eagen, and an examination of Fred's books will tell all.'

She hesitated. Then she spoke slowly and softly. 'I know why Roger robbed the bank and—'

'Stop, Laura!' cried Rathburn.

'No,' said Laura firmly; 'you may be going to prison.'

He put out one hand in protest.

Turning again to the sheriff she said:

'Roger did go to town last night, intending to give himself up. I knew he was going to do it by the way he looked at me. But today he saw me with Mr. Doane, and maybe he's heard things for which there was no warrant. Anyway, I know he thought I—I—was in love with Fred.'

'Laura—please!' Rathburn pleaded.

'And tonight,' said the girl in triumph, 'he heard Fred was cashier of the bank he'd robbed, and he brought the money back because he thought the robbery would hurt Fred and in that way hurt me!'

Rathburn turned appealingly to the sheriff 'Let's go,' he urged.

'He robbed that bank because he thought I had betrayed his trust, Sheriff Long!' cried Laura, her eyes shining.

'Are we going, Long?' cried Rathburn in an

agony.

The sheriff stepped to the door and called to some of his men who entered and bore the bodies of Doane and Eagen out of the sitting room. Then he took the money sack from the table and indicated to Rathburn to follow him, as he went out of the door. Rathburn went after him quickly, and the girl ran to the porch. Rathburn drew back with a cry, as he reached the porch. Just beyond the steps a horse was lying on its side.

'My—my hoss!' he cried wonderingly.

He leaped down beside the dead beast. Then he saw crimson upon the animal's shoulder, as a little gleam of light came from the door.

'That was why he jumped on the trail. He was hit. He carried me all this way with a bullet in him an' then dropped! One of Long's men shot him.'

Rathburn looked about vacantly. Then he sank down and buried his face on the shoulder of the dun, as Sheriff Long turned away. Laura Mallory stepped quickly to the side of the sheriff and touched his arm.

'Is he as bad as you think, sheriff?'

Long scowled at her in the dim light from the door, took out a thick, black cigar, bit the end off savagely, and began to chew it. He walked abruptly out to where some of his men were standing by their horses, and he said something in an undertone. When he returned, Rathburn had taken the saddle and bridle off the dead horse and was throwing the leather on the porch.

'Yours, dad,' he called to Mallory; 'I wouldn't use 'em again if I could.' Then he turned to the sheriff. 'All right, Bob.'

'Come inside,' said Long gruffly.

CHAPTER THIRTY-EIGHT

TEN MILES' START

When they were in the sitting room the sheriff confronted Rathburn.

'This has been a queer case for me,' he said slowly, with an attempt at harshness. 'I knew Eagen was up to a lot of dirty work, but I never could fasten anything on him till tonight. I'll get some of the rest of the gang now. Doane showed in his face that he was guilty. Those things don't worry me none. But *you* are the hardest character I ever had to handle, Rathburn!'

'I don't figure on givin' you any more trouble, sheriff,' Rathburn assured him, smiling.

'That's the puzzle of it!' Long exploded. 'That puts it up to me. I know you had reason for giving Gomez his, and I know this girl wouldn't lie about the other. But—well, I don't get you a-tall, Rathburn, and that's a fact. Something tells me I've got to give you a chance, and if I knew what tells me this I'd wring its neck!'

He stepped close to Rathburn and looked him straight in the eye.

'Take one of Mallory's horses. He's got some good ones. I give you ten miles in any direction. If you can make it—it's your candy. But remember, Rathburn, I'm going to try to stop you!'

He walked swiftly out of the door, leaving Rathburn staring at the smiling girl.

Laura stepped close to him and nodded. Rathburn shook his head.

'I can't see where I've got the right to give Long any more trouble.'

'But he isn't letting you go, Roger. He's putting it up to you, and he means what he says when he declares he'll try to get you.'

'If he does, he'll probably get me,' mused Rathburn.

'But maybe he won't get *us*, Roger.'

'Us?'

'You and I, Roger. Listen! There's a land 'way up north, Roger. I've read about it. It's past the desert and the mountains and the plains—in another country! And there's a river there, Roger—a river they call Peace River. I've always loved the name. We'll go there, Roger, you and I—and father can come later.'

She looked up at him with shining eyes and

put her arms about his neck, and she saw the unbelievable wonder in his face. The man trembled. Then he took her and held her and kissed her, time after time.

'Joe Price said I could never be satisfied away from the desert unless I took along something that was of it,' he muttered hoarsely; 'I wonder—'

'Yes, Roger, he meant me.'

'We can't make it,' he said softly. 'Not the two of us—but Laura, girlie, *this* is worth the game!'

'Yes we can, Roger,' she said eagerly. 'Think! We can be married when we've left the desert. It's not quite ten miles to Boxall Cañon. We can go up Boxall over the range and cross Death Flat.'

'I was thinking of that, sweetheart,' he replied. 'But no horse can get up Boxall, an' if he did he couldn't get across Death Flat. Few men have crossed that stretch. It's well named. I might try it alone; but you—no, Laura. It just ain't in the pictures!'

'We don't need horses, Roger. You've forgotten the burros. They'll kill any horse on the desert, won't they? We can take two or three loaded with food and water.'

'But it's miles and miles an' then some—an' it all looks alike.'

'But when we've reached the other side, Roger?'

He drew away from her and stepped to the

285

door. He could not see or hear anything. When he turned and again approached her, his face was white. He looked at Mallory, who was standing with a look of stupefaction on his lined face.

'Wait!' he said and stepped into another room. In a few moments he was back, holding a money belt in his hands. He took out gold and bills and deposited the money on the table.

The others stared.

'There's about six thousand there, Mallory. It's gamblin' money. Turn it in to the bank to make or help out Doane's shortage. I've got just twenty-five hundred left which I earned in a better way.'

'Daddy, get the burros!' cried the girl. 'We're going!'

*   *   *

Sheriff Bob Long looked down from a ledge above a narrow, deep, boulder-strewn, awe-inspiring cañon and drew in his breath sharply. Below he saw two human beings and three animals.

'I knew he'd try it,' Long said wonderingly to himself, 'I thought he'd try it afoot. But the girl! And they're going to try to cross Death Flat!'

His look of wonder increased, and he made no move toward the weapons in his holsters.

'I wonder now,' he mused. 'Can they make it? I wonder—'

He scowled and looked about with a frowning stare. His gaze again shifted downward. Suddenly he shrugged and put the wrong end of his unlighted cigar in his mouth.

'That's the queerest cigar I ever had,' he growled, as he made his way to his horse. 'It won't stay lit because it wants to be swallowed.'

He mounted and rode slowly back toward the far-reaching stretches of desert. Once he halted and turned in his saddle for a backward look.

'He had the makings of the worst bad man this country ever saw,' he muttered aloud. 'Now, if that woman and another country—but first they've got to get across.'

*   *   *

On the western edge of a great, ghastly plain of white, in which a deceiving, distant glow was mirrored in the desert dawn, two figures, a man and a girl, stood hand in hand. Three shaggy burros, heavily laden, stood behind them. The burros saw not the Death Flat ahead, for they were asleep.

And the man and the girl saw not the frightful white, as of powdered skulls, bare, sinister, sun-baked, but a vision of a little house in a fragrant green meadow, with golden

287

fields on either side of a peaceful river, and forests ranging up to distant hills.

APL		CCS	
Cen		Ear	
Mob		Cou	
ALL		Jub	
WH		CHE	
Ald	14/2/12	Bel	
Fin		Fol	
Can		STO	
Til		HCL	